A TASTE OF HONEY

A TASTE OF HONEY

A Taste of Honey

-A Novel Written by- LaTrice Allen

Copyright © 2014 by LaTrice Allen

Published by Bright Beginnings Publications

www.brightbeginningspublications.com

ISBN - 978-0-9862294-2-8

First Edition

Email: snickers0305@gmail.com

Follow on Instagram: @trixntreece

Follow on Twitter: @Sdyishoney

Cover design/Graphics: Michael Horne

Photographer: Ernest Wheeler

Model: Courtne Jones

Editor: Shalonda Johnson

Acknowledgements

I will try to make this short, LOL. First of all, all the glory goes to my Lord and Savior from delivering me from the darkness in my life and bringing me to a place of peace. There are so many people who were intricate parts of this journey, so please forgive me if I mistakenly omitted you from the acknowledgements, it was not my intention. To my sister, Renee, my cousins Nadyne and Sandi, thank you all for your proofreading, editing, comments, and endless support...I took everything with a grain of salt and my love for you all is endless. Courtney Parker, you have provided me with an unlimited amount of knowledge. Without your guidance I would not have been able to put this piece of work together and for that I am truly grateful. To my out of state 'sister girls', Sharla Showers (FL), Patricia Grijalva (NV) and Evadnie Felix (NY), I don't know what I would have done without our late night phone calls, my rants, my tears, and your consistent reassurance. Thank you ladies for being who you are and not holding back from our discussions, I love you all! I want to thank my bestie inner circle; Jane, Shontai, Cedric, Troy, Dana and Varick, y'all are my ride or dies...30 years of friendship cannot be measured by any means and your love, support and loyalty has meant the world to me, thanks for always being there, I love you all so much. Marlo you had to endure my stories for two years as we carpooled to work. Thank you for being a great friend and for listening and not jumping out the car, love you girl. To my 'Simply Read' sisters, thank you all for your encouragement and support you are the best book club sisters, no, you are the best sisters in the world! To the 'BookDivas,' you ladies are crazy as hell and I love you all. Tracey Todd, thank you for being 'Johnny on the spot.' You helped me out of some jams with deadlines and I can't thank you enough for that. Shalonda Johnson, my editor, you are a God send and I'm so happy to have you. I want to give a very special thanks to Vincent Wayne; my mentor and confidante. You have guided, directed, encouraged, and believed in me from the beginning. You are like a second father to me and I thank you from the bottom of my heart for always being there for me and believing in me. Trust me; you've had a huge impact in my life and played a major role to the woman I've become. Last but certainly not least, to all who have played a role in my past and my present, thank you. I need not name you...you know who you are. If it weren't for our life experiences, I would have not been able to create (A Taste of Honey) LOL; we've had some good times and created some wonderful memories, thank you for those memories, your support and for loving me for me! And for those in my future, I thank you in advance for the memories we will create.

Dedication

This book is dedicated to the love of my life, Courtne. Courtne you have been my life's inspiration from the moment I laid eyes on you. I knew being a mother was not going to be an easy job but the love you filled me with, made all the sacrifices, the tears, the heartache, and life's disappointments well worth it. With prayer, guidance, structure, communication and unconditional love, you have become the young woman I desperately prayed that you would be and then some. Words cannot express how much I love you...but you already know that!

A TASTE OF HONEY

A TASTE OF HONEY

BY

LATRICE ALLEN

Chapter one

Unfortunate events in my past, mainly my childhood, caused me to become numb to anything in life, other than the concept of making money. Sex became insignificant when I lost my virginity, and had my power and humanity robbed from me at the tender age of ten. Although the decision to have sex at ten clearly wasn't mine, I can't say the feeling I felt after D.J., my father's protégé, seven years my senior came inside me wasn't satisfying. Hell, D.J. was fine and I was fast; which when you combine the two, equals premature fucking. While growing up in our two-bedroom house, my mother was never one for much light. She would keep all the curtains drawn so no light could seep through. Our house was dark due to all the mayhem that went on. Looking back, it was probably best that none of the kids ever had full view of what was really happening. My father had a perfect hustle; there was an endless amount of traffic running through our home at any given time. Everyone wanted something from my dad; they craved a piece of him and he made sure he was available to meet their needs. I wanted something from my dad as well, his attention. Unfortunately, I never got the amount I needed. My father provided most of our neighborhood with drugs, alcohol, and wild parties. The majority of these events went on under our roof, making it a dangerous environment for me, my older sister Amber and my younger brother Justin. My curvaceous body came at an early age as did the attention from all of my father's friends. When my play uncle offered money to rub my booty, I didn't hesitate to snatch his money, in exchange for allowing him a quick feel. "Dirty Bastard," I'd say all the way to the bank, or rather the neck of my favorite doll, Cookie. I'd twist off her head and stuff the money inside. It didn't take long before word got out about my promiscuity. Soon, thereafter, five dollar feels turned into ten dollar fondling and eventually fifty dollar fucking. I made a great deal of money and unfortunately, Cookie's head was too small to hold all the cash I was bringing in. I had to relocate my stash of money from Cookie's head to a slit I made in my mattress. As the money rolled in, I quickly got to the point of not caring about the multitude of men parading around me; jockeying for my affections. Of course, I didn't care for any of these men as they were scumbags and I'd often wish for their demise. The only men that mean anything to me are: Benjamin, Andrew, Alexander, Abraham and George.

It's funny how genes work; my father was 6'4 and my mother was 5'11, and here I am at 5'5 on a good day. Amber is 5'9 and Justin is 6'6, go figure, and how is it that the middle child gets cheated on height. I love my smile, deep dimples, and light brown eyes with a touch of gold which I inherited all from my father. I'm basically a female version of him, not only his looks but my personality, attitude and business sense are identical as well. My skin is a caramel brown tone which makes my eyebrows and eyelashes stand out, due to their darkness and thickness. Instead of inheriting physical features from my mother, I inherited her gift of working my body in more ways than one. This feature has been a blessing and a curse. Don't get me wrong, my mother was an attractive woman, but due to her fast lifestyle, she got old before her time. When she met her unfortunate demise, she looked twenty years older and she was only thirty-nine. I guess the fast life with drugs, sex, and alcohol can do that to you. I'd watch through my slightly cracked bedroom door as my mother would perform for my dad and his friends. I observed her dancing and retained all of her moves. She was beautiful and her body was amazing; round plump butt, thick legs, small waist, and perky size 40 DDs even after three kids. When she danced it was like my father and his friends were dazed by her movements, just as I was. I thought to myself, when I grow up, I want to dance just like her. When no one was watching, I would try to emulate her moves. One time Amber caught me and grabbed me by the arm and told me, "little girls don't dance like that, so don't do it again". I knew she was mad at me because she gets very upset when my mother parades around men. My mother always wore a dress that flowed freely, giving her the flexibility to move about with no restrictions. I couldn't understand why my father and his friends would scream for her to continue to dance for hours on end. Her body moved like a feather floating through the air, light and delicate. Her hips moved from left to right; and she used her hands to touch her butt and breasts as she danced. When she did this, my father would stare at her in a way that made her do it more, it was like his stare was passing electricity to her which gave her more energy. The men in the room would go crazy, screaming and clapping. She would close her eyes and her head would sway from side to side. I think she went to another place. She'd slightly part her legs, taking her hand to caress her "centerpiece", my dad and his friends would go wild screaming things like, "work it baby", "and let me see what you're working with." I'd watch in amazement how my mother moved so gracefully and how she made all the men including my father scream for more. I'm going to be just like my mother I said to myself. I watched a ballerina on T.V. once and thought my mother was just as beautiful as she was and that she moved just as gracefully. Both my mother and the ballerina were one and the same; they moved their bodies from side to side, closed their eyes as they danced, used their arms to touch their bodies, kicked their legs high, and had people screaming for more. The ballerina performed for a crowd of people who loved the art of ballet and my mother performed for a crowd of people who loved being thugs, dope heads, and child molesters! Little did I know, the fruit didn't fall too far from the tree, and that I too would make my body move with such grace, use my hands to caress my body, kick my legs high, and have men screaming for more! It's genetic. It's in my blood and my wish of being like my mother came true.

I studied my father as well. Many feared him. His presence sent a message that he was not to be crossed. He made a name for himself in the streets long before we were born. I've heard stories of people he killed, fights he had where men were unable to walk or talk again. People called him "Killer" on the streets. He feared no one but many feared him and would never challenge him. My father also had a gentle side, well at least with me and my siblings. He loved my mother, there was no doubt about that, but the drugs and alcohol took him over many times, coming home from his wild nights out with his biker friends and would beat my mother to no end, for no reason. She quickly learned that if she was out with him, she could control his intake and possibly minimize the beatings. I never understood why someone would stay with a person who caused them harm and pain. I guess I didn't understand love or at least what I thought love was because I was young. My father never laid a hand on us, he'd give us that look, and we knew to get it together or else. My mother on the other hand, had no problem smacking us when needed or when she was pissed off that my father wouldn't let her roll with him. As children we saw more than any child should see, and experienced so much tragedy at such young ages. My mother and father were killed when I was twelve, Amber was sixteen, and Justin was nine. Due to their lifestyle it was unenviable that our world would come crashing down. After their deaths, Amber had no choice but to grow up even more and take on the role of me and Justin's guardian and take care of us. My father told Amber that if anything ever happened to him, that he had enough money hidden for us to live on. She retrieved his stash and made sure we had somewhere to live, food to eat, and clothes on our backs. Amber was smart and was able to make the undisclosed amount of money last for years. My parents loved all three of us, I'm sure; however, it was clear that my father loved us more, making sure we'd be okay if he left this earth. I'm sure providing for us was not on my mother's mind. All she was concerned with was making my father happy and running the streets. I remember my brother drinking beer with the men while my sister and I sat on some man's lap who we always called "uncle". Two of these so-called uncles were doing things to me and Amber no uncle should be doing. One particular night, I remember like it was yesterday. I wish these memories would go away but for some reason they won't. Amber had just finished taking her shower; she flips the toilet down and sits on it to dry off with her giant purple bath towel. When she steps out the shower, I step in. We both are singing and are happy as we could be. I step out of the shower and she hands me a giant red bath towel. I tell her, "You got out first so you can have the purple towel," she laughs and says, "Yep, sure did." I roll the tip of the towel and twirl it around in the air to try to slap her legs with it. We were startled by a knock on the bathroom door. Amber yells, "We're almost done." There was no reply. After we both were dry, we wrap our towels around our bodies. Amber opens the bathroom door, peeks out, turns back to me and says, "The coast is clear, come on." We walk out the bathroom holding our towels around our bodies and make our way to our bedroom. Just as we enter the bedroom, Amber quickly tries to close the bedroom door, but it seems to be blocked by something. She tries to force it close, when she looks down to see a big black steel toe boot blocking the door. The door flings open, and Amber stumbles trying not to fall. Uncle Luke is standing in the doorway now. "Uncle Luke, what are you doing in here?" Amber asks with a shaky voice and a look of concern on her face. Uncle Luke steps further in the room and shuts the door behind him. He says nothing for a moment and has a deranged look on his face, a look of a crazy man. This frightened Amber and I. Justin was in the room but under the covers on the bottom bunk, asleep or so we thought. Uncle Luke told us to "drop our towels" and let him "take a look at our pretty little bodies." "You must be out of your mind if you think I am going to let your nasty ass look at me and my sister. It's not happening," Amber shouts! Amber tries to walk pass him to get to the bedroom door to cry out for help. He grabs her, flings her back with a slight nudge and she falls to the floor. She quickly gets up and stands in front of me, trying to protect me. Amber knows she is no match for Uncle Luke and is frantically thinking of a way out. She has no idea what he is about to do, so she must think fast. We can tell Uncle Luke is drunk because the smell of booze is seeping out of his pores. Amber says, "If you don't leave this room right now, I am going to scream and my daddy, Killer, as you call him, will be in here with a quickness to see what's wrong. I don't think your ass wants to fuck with my daddy, now do you?" I look at my sister surprised because she was cussing at a grown-up. Uncle Luke looks surprised as well and says, "Well look here, the smart one has a potty mouth and I'm not worried about Killer for your information. Call your daddy, baby girl. You hear that music and laughter out there? You think he's going to hear you? Go on and give it your best shot." Amber screams to the top of her lungs. She screams so loud that it scares Justin; he jumps, but stays under the covers. He peeks his head from up under the covers to see what was going on and when he saw Uncle Luke in the room, he put his head back under the covers. Unfortunately, her screams went unheard.

Uncle Luke says, "See, I told you he wouldn't hear you, now do what I said and both of you remove the damn towels. Hey, little mama I need you to drop yours first. I've been watching you and you are developing into a fine little thing. I can tell your little ass is gonna be fine as hell when you get older." My sister stood her ground and said, "Over my dead body!" Uncle Luke laughs and says, "Wow potty mouth, you got balls too, I admire that, you sure is your daddy's child." He wipes that evil smile off his face and says, "That can be arranged potty mouth." He pulls out a gun from behind his leather vest. He holds the gun in his hand and stares at us for a second, and then he yells, "Little mama, come here!" My sister slightly pushed me back and says, "Leave her alone, I'm coming." As my sister heads towards him he says, "That's what I'm talking about; bring your smart ass mouth over here." Uncle Luke turns around and lays the gun on the dresser behind him next to the bunk bed, then reaches for a chair that was in the far right corner and sat down in the middle of the room. Amber stands in front of him and he reaches to remove the bath towel that was wrapped around her small frame. The towel hit the floor and I start to cry. At that moment, the music stopped, but I still heard laughter; I thought about screaming but knew no one would hear me and I was afraid Uncle Luke was going to shoot us. I knew this was not going to be good. I look over at the bottom bunk and see Justin moving, crawling towards the dresser. Uncle Luke was not paying attention to the movement in the bunkbed because his eyes are focused on my Amber. To tell you the truth, I don't think Uncle Luke knew he was in the room. He was too busy thinking of a way he could take advantage of us. He reaches out to touch her breast when Justin yells, "Leave my sisters alone!" Uncle Luke quickly turned around to see Justin standing behind him pointing the gun right at his belly. "Hey little buddy, I need you to give me that gun before someone gets hurt," he says. Justin yells, "You are the one who's gonna get hurt if you don't get out of our room and leave my sisters alone." My little brother's demands went unanswered. Uncle Luke turns to my sister and grabs her breast. "I said leave my sisters alone, Uncle Luke!" Justin yells. Gunshots rang out. Bang! Bang! Bang! Justin shot

Uncle Luke 3 times, one bullet hit him in the back that exited his stomach, another hit him in the back of his head and the last went through his chest, hitting his heart. All of a sudden, the bedroom door burst open and in comes my daddy. I'm standing in the corner in a puddle of my own urine shaking uncontrollably. Amber is still standing butt naked as the day she was born with blood and body matter splattered all over the front of her body and Justin stands frozen like a statue still holding the gun in his hands. This was the beginning of the end for Justin's troubled life. With all the shit we went through and saw as children, I'm surprised we aren't more screwed up than we are.

Chapter two

The stale smell of cigarettes, hot ass and sweaty men, float through the air and makes my stomach turn. The pea green walls looks like someone covered them with sweet peas from a jar of Gerber's baby food. My dressing room is depressing but at least I don't have to share my space with the other dancers. The walls are made of cement, dull, cold, and resemble a jail cell. The only thing different is the jail cell gate is replaced with a weak, brown wooden door that squeaks when opened or closed. I look past my dressing room's ugliness and focus on the task at hand...making money. The other dancers share a large room with lockers and eight tables with surrounding lights, something like a make-shift vanity. The room reminds me of a high school girl's locker room, very basic and gloomy. I make it a point to be here on time, the less time I spend in this room the better I feel. I give myself just enough time to get prepared so I don't waste time in my dressing room or have idle chit-chat with these heffas! One cannot be the star and not have haters. They all talk to me then talk about me. When you get to be as good as I am, haters are a part of the game. I have brains, beauty, I'm sophisticated and mysterious.....which clearly sets me apart from the other dancers. I'm surprised I don't have more haters than I do. I constantly remind myself of the song by the O'Jays, "*They smile in your face, all the while they want to take your place, the backstabbers*". Well, welcome to my world! I carefully apply my makeup, making sure my face is flawless. I stare at myself in the mirror and I am pleased at what I see, at least from the outside. But, as I continue to stare at myself, sadness comes over me and I quickly look away because the woman staring back at me has an empty and blank expression that scares me. At this point, I no longer like what I see. I turn from the mirror and step away from my vanity. I walk towards my dressing room closet to retrieve my opening act costume. Once my costume is on, I close the door so I can have access to the full length mirror on the back of the door. I glance at myself from head-to-toe to make sure I am 100% together as I only have a few more minutes before it's time to hit the stage. I look at the big clock on the wall; it reads 9:58pm. I take one more look at myself in the mirror, slightly rub my lips together and say another prayer. I stand, head towards the exit ready to become every man's fantasy. The music is blaring. I hear "Shake What Yo Mama Gave Ya", and that's my cue to hit the stage. I open the door, click off the light, lock the bottom door knob, and close it shut behind me. I leave Sydney in the dressing room and it is time for, Honey, to hit the stage. The club is packed, and the club goers are ready to spend some money. It's dark in the club, the tables are filled with men and women laughing, drinking, and bobbing their heads to the blaring music coming from the speakers that surround the clubs walls. There's a catwalk-like stage in the middle of the club with a number of tables and chairs on either side. A spotlight shines on the pole in the middle of the stage. I give my cue to the DJ by nodding my head and he announces, "Alright y'all, the moment we've all been waiting for, the honey is spilling out the jar tonight. Please show some love for our superstar of the evening, HONEY," he yells. I walk out towards the stage and the room explodes. I hear people yelling and screaming my name, clapping their hands and whistling. I look around as I walk through the club making my way to the stage. I see some dazed stares and I laugh to myself. I flaunt my stuff like I am a high-priced model; on a catwalk at a fashion show in London. My black lace bodysuit with the ass and the crouch missing is killer and sure to keep all eyes on me. I reach the stage, turn my back to the crowd and drop into a squat just as the spotlight is now directly on me. Squatting, my legs are spread wide, and I gently place my hands on my parted knees and begin to flex my butt cheek muscles. First, I bounce the right cheek muscle to the beat of the music, then the left cheek, then I switch between the two (right, left, right, left) at that moment the club interrupts with louder screams, hand claps, and whistles. This is just what I need to fuel my fire. The music starts to fade and I stand and turn to face the crowd. I pose, take a deep breath and wait for the music to change. I see some of my regulars and I also see some fresh meat in the house, so I make a mental note to make my way to their seats... they look like some big spenders. I think to myself.....Showtime! I hear someone scream "I sure would love some of that honey on my face tonight!" Again, more fuel. The next song cues in; Aaliyah's "I Care for You" softly drifts through the speakers. I have an extensive athletic background; track, swimming, dance, gymnastics, and cheerleading. This training gives me the ability to move and create a fantasy that drives the crowd wild and sets me apart from the rest. I turn slowly, walk over to the pole and hold on to it like it's my man, gently stroking it, caressing it like it's a ten foot dick. Even though the music is playing, it's quiet, no one says a word, and every eye is glued to me as I give them a mesmerizing and captivating performance. I notice a man standing at the edge of the stage with his eyes glued to my every move. His mouth is slightly ajar and he stands like a mannequin, not moving a muscle.

I return the stare. I don't remove my eyes from his, slowly dropping to the floor all the while still holding and stroking the pole. He blinks and swallows. I smile inside because he's obviously captivated by my performance and I have him under my spell. It feels good to know that these men throw, toss, and gently place their hard-earned money on the stage all the while wishing that the pole I'm stroking is in fact their dicks. I focus back on mannequin man at the foot of the stage still standing there looking like he lost his puppy. I finish my seductive dance, and crawl over to him. I get close to him and he moves and whispers the words, "fuck me". I don't know if he meant that literally or figuratively, doesn't matter because I have one goal in mind and that is to make sure the wad of bills he holds in his sweaty little hands will go home with me tonight! I stand as I reach the end of the stage, he looks up at me and I wink which makes him smile. He stands at least six feet tall, has a shaved head with flawless milk chocolate skin. By me standing on the stage and wearing 7" heels, his face is aimed right at my center-piece. I place my hands on both sides of his head and gently pull his head closer to me. He's stiff but quickly relaxes and lets me guide his face between my legs. I move my hips in a circular motion, not letting go of his head. I can feel his warm breath between my legs as he inhales, then exhales. I let his head go before poor mannequin man has a major nut in front of the crowd, not that he would care because he was truly in heaven. I turn around and bend over grabbing my ankles; my butt is directly in his face. I'm staring at him through my legs and he reaches up and places a folded bill at my ankle under my bodysuit. I pull the bill out with my teeth, stand and face him. I squat so I can be somewhat at eye level with him and push the bill further in my mouth. Once I get the bill in my mouth, I tie it in a knot with my tongue, just like a cherry stem. I reach up to my mouth to retrieve the bill and display another one of my talents. He smiles and leans close to my ear and whispers, "Impressive". I reply, "Indeed." The song is coming to an end and at that time mannequin man makes it rain, leaving every bill in his hand at my feet. I lean over and kiss his sweaty forehead and whisper, "Thanks honey." I think to myself, another mesmerizing performance and satisfied customer. I bring my performance to a close so I can step off the stage and make some real money with lap dances, private dances, and, if it's a good night a little something extra. "Give Miss Honey a hand for that wonderful performance!" the DJ shouts into the mic. The room explodes with applause. I feel so good knowing that I have yet again pleased so many men with my performance. I step off the stage, heading to my dressing room to freshen up and change, when a hand grabs me by the arm. I turn to see who has such a tight hold on me. These are the times I wish Justin were here to have my back. When I turn around to see who has the nerve to touch me, it is my worst nightmare: my ex-boyfriend Cameron. He has, once again, reared his ugly head. He is not ugly in the sense of bad looking; this is not the case at all. Cameron has the beautiful looks that I am so attracted to: "BBB" big, black, and bald! Cameron is a pro-football player for the San Francisco Tigers. Standing 6'3 and about two-hundred and twenty pounds; his skin the color of a dark, creamy Hershey Milk Chocolate Candy Bar, makes my mouth water whenever I think about it. Cameron and I were a hot item for about a year. Things were wonderful so I thought. He had his football thing and I had my dancing thing of which he liked.... at the time. One night, Cameron and I were at Club Delaney's, and the owner of the club, Delaney, had approached and suggested I dance, from a previous conversation we had about how I love to dance. Cameron seemed ok about it. He and Delaney went way back, so Cameron knew I would be in good hands. He encouraged me to be the best damn dancer I could be, and that's what I did. He was my biggest fan. He would throw me the most money because it was a game for him. He wanted to see if anyone would match making it rain on me because, believe me, he made it perfectly clear to anyone who came near me that I was his and they'd better back the hell up.

When men started to match his dollars, he had a big problem. I should have picked up on his possessiveness, but I was blinded by his fame, all the money, glam, and all the other perks that came along with it. If he only knew about half the dudes in our circle that were trying to get at me, he would have busted a blood vessel. Things were just peachy keen in the beginning of my dancing career, but as I became the most popular dancer in a very short period of time, Cameron started to feel threatened. He made comments like, "you don't need to dance anymore," "I take good care of you and give you everything you need and want." "This club is wack, and ain't nothing up in here but a bunch of busters. Plus I don't like the punk ass bitches looking at my woman," you know, shit like that. Yeah, I dismissed the signs. The more I ignored him and his comments, the angrier he became. He started demanding that I quit or else. That fool had to have forgotten who the hell I was. I know I am no match for a linebacker, but I have something that would have stopped that motherfucker if he ever imagined laying a hand on me. Don't fuck with me, fool, I'm from Compton and the fool will be "Casket Sharp" before his time if he ever put his hands on me. I'm not sure if I truly loved Cameron, but I did love the fact that he could take care of me, financially and in the bedroom. Don't get me wrong, I clear anywhere from four to six thousand dollars a weekend dancing. It is not close to what Cameron is making but I'd say I'm doing okay. The best part about Cameron is that he puts it down in the bedroom. He is all man and I really loved every inch of his athletic build. I loved his chest and six pack. His arms were to die for, and I loved holding on to them. His legs were toned but not big like Mighty Mouse and his ass was perfectly round. The best part about his body was his "Package"! Cameron has what every man wishes he were blessed with, a 9-½ inch rod iron pole that curves to the left. His package was perfect for hitting all the right spots. I called it 'BLT', black, long and thick! Cameron was blessed with a talent in the bedroom which is why we were so compatible. He met his match, when he met me. I can't honestly say that Cameron and I ever made love. I can't recall if I have ever made love, believe me, when I do, you will be the first to know. What Cameron and I did was fuck. Fucking is something both of us love and he hung with my hearty sexual appetite. We're both in the business of pleasing each other which, in the end, was not a good idea for us to be together. Cameron began to follow me around. He had other people giving him reports on what I was doing and where I was going. I became an obsession and a possession to him, which I hated because I don't fucking belong or answer to no one but myself. I don't give a shit who you are. When he grabbed me that night at the club and told me, "If I can't have you then no one can." I knew it was time to cut his ass loose.

I told Cameron to let go of my arm. He insisted on speaking to me but I refused because I was working. "Sydney I need to talk to you," he says. "Not now, I'm working and I don't have time for this shit right now," I reply. He pulls me closer, through clenched teeth and says "I need to talk to you NOW!" The look on my face tells Rocky, the club's bouncer and my best friend that I need some assistance and right now. As Rocky approaches us, Cameron loosened his grip a bit. "Hey man, Honey is working and this is not the time or place for this nonsense so why don't you let her go right now," Rocky says. Without hesitation, Cameron let go of my arm, and he is clearly upset that Rocky has intervened. Cameron stares into my eyes, and says, "Syd, *this* is not over!"

Chapter three

Time is of the essence, and I am losing money wasting time with Cameron. I head to the back to freshen up so I can go work the room. It's one of my favorite parts of the night. I also enjoy conversing with the customers. Working the room is another way of making my money. I dance in the aisles; I perform lap dances, allow men to stare at my ass, and provide private dances, all for the love of money. It takes me a minute to relax before I can go back out there and make more money. Hopefully no one saw what went down with Cameron. I'd hate to have someone second-guess their plans to hook up with me tonight. I slowly peel off my two-piece black outfit and glance over at the closet to remind myself what outfits I had pulled out earlier for this evening. After I remove my clothes and shoes, I walk over to the closet and decide to put on a white one-piece lace body suit with a hot pink push-up bra and a pair of hot pink G-strings. I put on a pair of hot pink "come fuck me pumps", put on my honey face and head back to take care of my business. As I walk around the club, I see some of my regulars. My regulars are consistent with lap dances. The majority of them do not purchase private dances because they don't want to spend the money. A customer taps me on the shoulder and slightly grabs my hand, to have me stand in front of him. He smiles and says, "I need a lap dance from you tonight Honey." I return the smile and move a little closer to him. The music is blaring through the speakers, and my body feels the beat of the music and I start to move to the beat. He sits in his chair; I take my hands and pull his legs together, so it's easier for me to straddle him. I turn around with my back facing him and start to move my hips and grind my centerpiece against his legs. His hands rise to cup my butt. I take my left hand and smack his hands away from my butt. I turn my head to make eye contact with him to let him know he is breaking the rules by putting his hands on my ass. I move forward and turn to face him, and he looks like he's a bit buzzed and maybe even drunk, but I move closer to straddle him from the front. As I do my thing, a regular is looking at me like I am a plate of chicken and waffles, and he can't wait to sop me up and eat me. My customer reaches in his right back pocket and pulls out a small money clip. He removes two fifty dollar bills and places the money clip back in his pocket. He then takes one of the fifties and folds it in half, the long way. With the fifty dollar bill, he takes the bill and starts to trace a circle up my thighs. It tickles, so I smile. He probably thinks he's turning me on with his weak ass attempt of seduction. He reaches the trim of my thong and places the bill in my panties. He then repeats this little gesture once again; placing the other fifty in my panties. I kiss him on the forehead then move close to his ear and tell him "thank you". As I pull away from him, he smiles at me then says, no, "thank *you* Honey". I love my regulars they always take care of me. Some of my regulars are really sweet guys and a few want to get with me but outside of the club I have a golden rule: I don't shit where I sleep. Furthermore I'm a true believer of Usher's song "Pro Lover" which clearly states:

"loving me baby that's a no-no; I'm better when I touch and go, I'm trying to add your name to my hall of fame; not just a player, I'm a pro."

As long as I follow these words, I'm good. I move on to another customer for a lap dance and I notice a gorgeous man across the room checking me out. I glanced at him while I was doing my thing on the stage. He studied my every move, not taking his eyes off me once. While dancing, I lock eyes with him; giving him a look like, yeah I will screw your brains out. I winked at him but he doesn't react. He just kept staring at me. After this lap dance, I need to make my way over to him and give him a lap dance on the house because this man is fine as hell. I tuck my money in my bra as our eyes lock. As I head in his direction, Rocky intercepts me and whispers in my ear, "You have a private dance waiting in the back room for you." Shit, I really want to see what ole boy is about but it will have to wait because I have to make my money. I turn towards the back room. My private dances start at a thousand dollars and go up depending on the type of dance/service I provide. I am selective about who I show special treatment. Some people may call me a hoe...call me what you like. One, because I don't give a shit, and two, because I'd like to see these bitches make as much money as I do. Dancing at the club is extra money because I make the majority of my money outside the club, that's another story for a later date. I glance back at the mystery man and shrug my shoulder. He tips his glass, slightly bows his head to the side and smiles. I damn near melt. I feel like a stick of butter that has been placed in a hot skillet, hot and sizzling. I think to myself, this *"muthafucka"* is fine as hell. I lean into Rocky, "See that dude over there?" Rocky shakes his head yes. "Please go over there and tell him Honey said don't leave. Tell him I have something for him." Rocky calmly walks over to him and does as he's told. The mystery man tips his glass, slightly bows his head to the side and smiles. "Damn he did it again," I whisper to myself. He gives me a seductive smile. I melt again but my centerpiece tingles, getting slightly moist. I think, "Who is this dude? I don't know but I will damn sure find out!" Something about this mystery man intrigues me. I make my way to the private dance room to make my money. I open the door, walk in, and close the door behind me. I am shocked to see who is sitting in the large, high-back chair waiting for my arrival. It's one of the Bay area's finest, a center for the Sacramento Jaguars, and one of my favorite basketball players, DeVon Simpson. I smile and say, "Well, well, well, this is a surprise." DeVon is 6'10 and two-hundred and twenty pounds of pure steel! He has several tattoos on his arms and chest, and he is sexy as hell. It's something about an athlete with an abundance of tattoos all over his body; the shit is a major turn-on for me. This man is exactly how I like my men: BBB. He's not as thick as Cameron, mainly because of the height difference, but I'm sure he can still put it down, or at least I hope he can. If he can't, I am going to be so disappointed. I've always had a crush on him and I have fantasized often about getting him into my bed! This just might be his lucky night. I walk over to him, extend my hand and say, "Hello, my name is Honey." He looks up at me with this devilish smile and in a deep sexy, radio DJ, kind of voice replies, "I know exactly who you are." "Okay mister; let's skip the formalities, what's your pleasure?" I ask. "I want to know if you really taste like honey," he responds. I think to myself, "Oh, yeah, this is going to be his lucky night!" I smile and say, "This will cost you." He looks at me with his devilish smile again and asks "How much?" I place my finger next to my mouth like I'm thinking about it and say, "Let's see, twenty-five hundred?" He looks at me and answers, "I'll make you a deal." "Speak," was my response. He then says, "If you really taste like honey, I'll give you thirty-five hundred with the agreement I can come back for more whenever I like." I chuckle, "you got a deal mister. He looks at me long and hard like he's undressing me with his eyes and imagining what he wants to do to me. Well if he's undressing me with his eyes, this shouldn't take long; because I don't have too much on. I match his stare for what seems like forever. Finally, he stands and moves close to me. I try to back up a little, allowing some space between us but there's no room for me to do that. I can't move because he has me pinned against the wall. DeVon looks down at me, places his large hands under my arms, lifts me off the floor, and requests that I wrap my legs around his waist, I comply. He lowers his lips to mine, then slowly plants small sensual kisses on my lips. I close my eyes as this man is turning me on! His tongue gently slides in my mouth, and my tongue is eager to meet his. As our tongues meet, we automatically connect and lustfully they dance in our mouths like we're performing the tango on Dancing with the Stars. My centerpiece is moist with anticipation of what's coming next. DeVon stops kissing me and gently puts me down. His gaze meets mine once again. He lifts my chin, and then plants soft kisses on my cheeks. His tongue outlines both of my dimples. I think to myself, "this brother has smooth skills and it's making me hotter than a wildfire on a hillside; burning out of control." He pushes my back up against the counter, and with one move turns me around so that I can see myself in the mirror. My back is turned towards him. I throw my hands up in the air and think *alright*! His hands caress my breasts, and then they examine the curves of my body. His hands move up and down my butt and legs, as he's kissing me down my back, which is driving me crazy because he is also tracing the tattoo of my honey jar with his tongue. At this point, I am going crazy because this is one of my hot spots. Before I know it, he's on the floor with his face looking directly at my centerpiece. "Don't say a word," he says. I nod in agreement. We find a comfortable position; he's basically sitting under me, with his face smothered between my legs. He catches me off guard, moves my thong to the side, and proceeds to flick his tongue on my love button. "Okay, Mr. Sacramento Jaguar forward, work your magic. Do the damn thing." And the damn thing is exactly what he did. "Oh My", I said.

He stops and says, "I told you not to say a word." "I'm so sorry, please continue," I reply. As I am bent over the counter, he inserts his finger into my wet heaven. He continues to suck my clit as his finger is massaging my g-spot. The way he's sucking me is making me lose control. I feel my body about to erupt. My toes curl, my eyes roll in the back of my head, and I let go of the most powerful orgasm I have ever experienced. As I came, my juices were trying to escape but DeVon made sure he drank every last drop. When he's done, he stands, picks up a hand towel that is nicely folded on the counter and wipes his mouth. He then reaches into his pocket and pulls out a large bundle of cash. He places the cash on the table. He walks towards the door, turns to me and says, "Nice to

TASTE you, Honey." DeVon walks out the door but before leaving he says, "Until next time, stay sweet, Honey." I am dumbfounded and somewhat in a state of shock: this man just put some shit on me I have never experienced before. I have had many a men's tongues between my legs, but I have never had a man eat me like this! All I can say is that he ate me like I was his last meal! Ole boy worked his tongue like a dentist works his drill, like a surgeon works his scalpel, and like an artist works his paintbrush. Shit, you get the idea. DAMN! I counted the money on the table, four thousand dollars: I throw my hands in the air and shout out loud, "ALRIGHT!" I am on cloud nine, feeling like a million bucks, I can't stop smiling and I am still tingling with excitement. "Oh shit, my mystery man", I forgot about him; I thought. I quickly freshen up, fix my hair and make-up, change my outfit, and make my way back into the club. I need to see that gorgeous man who was giving me his undivided attention. As I walk out, a few more customers stop me for a lap dance, but I refuse because I need to get to my mystery man. I finally make it over to the other side of the room where he was but he's gone. I looked all over the club. "I hope he's in the men's room," I whisper. I have a feeling he left for the night. I am really disappointed that I did not get to meet, let alone, talk to this mystery man. I hope he comes back. I dance a few more lap dances, shoot the shit with a few people, and then head to the back to my dressing room to change. After I refresh, I count my earnings and I'm pleased. I grab my bag and make my way to the exit. Once I exit my room, the club is near empty, and a few customers remain with the waitresses, and the clean-up crew. I walk over to Delaney and hand him an envelope with my portion of tonight's earnings. Most girls pay him twenty-five percent of their earnings, but Cameron negotiated a better deal for me: the most I pay is ten percent. I make more money than all the other girls combined, so Delaney never complains because the amount is always substantial. He takes his cut and smiles. Tonight was a good night, clearing six thousand dollars; I give Delaney a little extra. "Good night as always Hon, be safe and see you next week," he says. I bend over; give him a peck on the cheek and say, "you do the same boss." "Do you need me to walk you to your car?" I laughed to myself because Delaney is a little white man about 5'2 with hazel eyes, thick grey hair and mustache and the biggest heart anyone could have. What is he going to do if someone approaches us in the parking lot? I don't know and I didn't want to find out. Rocky is always packing and so is Delaney, but I'd rather take my chances with Rocky. "No, Delaney, Rocky will walk me out," I say as I wait for Rocky to stop talking to this hoochie mama. I wait another fifteen minutes while Rocky gets his mack on. I walk over to him, "Give her your number, or get hers so y'all can continue this conversation at a later time. I'm tired and really want to go home." I express. Rocky did as I suggested, writes his number on a napkin and hands it to ole girl. "Call me." She smiles as she hands him her number, "Will do," she sings. Rocky is a sweetheart. He and I connected right away, and he always has my back. He knows my brother and promised he would take care of me until he returns home; he's away on vacation, if you know what I mean. Justin and Rocky became pretty close and when he got locked up a few months ago, Rocky told Justin not to worry about me that he would take over the brother role until his return. Rocky is a big teddy bear, I guess like most club bouncers. He's 6'3 and large but his body is in proportion for his height and weight. Rocky reminds me of Gerald LeVert because of the way he looks and sings. He can blow and mesmerizes women with his voice the same way I hypnotize men with my dancing. Sometimes when we're alone in the club, Rocky will sing and I get on the stage, close my eyes, dance and let Rocky's baritone sultry voice take me to another place. Rocky is a cutie pie and I love him because he has a heart of gold. Justin hung out at the club, a little weird, by the way, to have your little brother hang out at a club where you're naked and dancing with strange men, but he didn't trip because he was there to make sure the customers didn't get out of hand and wanted me to make my money.

Chapter four

Rocky grabs his coat and we head for the parking lot. A few cars remain in the lot. I feel a weird flutter in my stomach that Cameron hasn't left and that he is waiting for me. I turn to Rocky and say, "I think Cameron is still here. He did tell me it was not over between us." Rocky pulls his gun out from behind his jacket, a 45 automatic, and quickly scans the parking lot and the surrounding areas. "I don't see his car. I'll follow you home to make sure you get in safely. I don't want you to have any unwanted guest," he expressed. "Thanks," I say as we get into our cars, drive off, and head towards the Bay Bridge to San Francisco. I live in a high-rise apartment building right on the bay in San Francisco. I love my apartment and being on the 18th floor gives me a wonderful view of the Bay and the Golden Gate Bridge that's viewable from the large window in my living room. The apartment building comes with a door man named Stanley. Stanley is in his fifties and a Caucasian man of average height and weight. I'm not sure where he is from because he has a thick accent, maybe Australia or Ireland. I think it's cute and I can understand him perfectly. I always give him nice holiday gifts because he is such a sweet man. Whenever I walk through the front door, Stanley nods his head, touches the tip of his hat and says "Good day Ms. Sydney." He updates me on his family, his children, and he lights up like a Christmas tree when he talks about them. If there's a God up there, maybe one day I will have a family that makes me light up when I speak of them. Oh well, stop dreaming "Honey," I whisper, because it's not in the cards for you to have a husband or a family. Rocky drives into the carport behind me. I pull my black-on-black convertible 6 series BMW into my designated spot and Rocky pulls his cream colored Cadillac Escalade into the visitor's spot. We exit our cars and walk to the elevator. Rocky pushes the up button on the elevator to bring it down to the parking garage. We enter the elevator; I slide my key card in and push the 18th floor. I feel somewhat safe in my building but if someone really wants to get in and get to me, they can. We step off the elevator and head to my apartment door and all looks normal. I wiggle my key in the door. Before I open it, my two baby boys come running and barking. I have a 5-year-old cocker spaniel mix named Snickers and a 3-year-old toy poodle named Teddy. These two, outside of my brother and sister are the loves of my life. Rocky enters first and pats the boys on the head and talks some doggy Rocky talk. "Hey Snicker Doodle and Teddy Bear, how's Uncle Rocky's boys doing?" he says, in his goo-goo, ga-ga, baby voice. It's funny as hell to hear because he is so big, and he's using the baby talk to talk to the dogs. He checks each room in the apartment and yells, "It's all good Honey." As he turns to leave, I ask, "Do you have plans for the night? Do you mind staying with me because I don't want to be alone tonight." "I'm free. I'll stay with you. What do you have to eat sis because a brother sure is hungry." I laugh because he sounds like "Brotha Man from the 5th floor" on *Martin*. "The fridge is filled with food, have at it. I'm going to take a shower," I reply. In the shower, I'm thinking Rocky and I can pop some popcorn and watch a movie. I slide into my PJ's and head to the living room where I witness a Kodak moment: Snickers, Teddy, and Rocky are curled on the floor knocked out next to each other. If only I had a camera to snap a picture, because no one will ever believe me if I told them this big fool was lying on the floor, curled up with two little dogs. Priceless! I lie in the bed; looking at the ceiling, thinking about what I am going to do today. What am I going to cook for dinner? How can I think about what to cook for dinner when I haven't even had breakfast yet? That's me, always thinking ahead. I realize I haven't heard from my sister in a few days. I will give her a call once I get up and start moving around. We generally talk every day. I need to roll out of the bed so I can take the boys for a walk, but I just can't find the strength to move right now. My body is tired and I feel like I just need to rest. There is a teenager named Brandy, who lives on the 3rd floor, who sometimes walks the boys for me when I am tired or out of town. I'll call her to see if she can take Snickers and Teddy out before they mess in the house. I look at the clock on my nightstand; it reads 10:26am. Okay, Sydney, get your ass out the bed and get a move on it, I think. Normally, I don't sleep this late because the boys usually jump on my bed, bark, or do something they have no business doing to get my attention. Speaking of the boys jumping and barking, it's too quiet and I panic. Then I remember Rocky fell asleep with them last night, and I closed my bedroom door, because Rocky was snoring so loudly that I thought a herd of hogs were going to run through my apartment at any moment. Calling the hogs is an understatement, when it comes to Rocky's snoring. I quickly jump up and out of my bed to open my bedroom door to hear nothing, why is it so quiet? I walk into the living room to find a note on the coffee table:

I picked up some breakfast from Denny's and bought you a mocha latte from Coffee Bean. It's in the microwave ready for you to eat when you're ready. I'm taking Mr. Snicker Doodle and Mr. Teddy Bear for a drive to get them out of the house for a while and to give you a chance to get some peace and quiet. By the way, you really need to think about getting Teddy some type of discipline training because he is bad as hell. He punks poor Snickers to death. Also, you owe me a new pair of shoes because Teddy decided to give them a few extra holes. And yes, I know it was Teddy because I opened my eyes this morning to the sound of fine Italian leather being chewed. I caught him in mid-chew and he looked at me like "oh shit I'm busted." He let go of the shoe and dodged under the dining room table. Yeah, he knew he was in trouble. Anyway, call me when you're ready for me to bring Snickers and Billy Bad Ass home.

Love, Rocky.

I laugh out loud because I know how bad Teddy is. He's so damn cute with those big brown puppy dog eyes that get me every time. I am so grateful for the relationship I have with Rocky. He loves and takes such good care of me. He is truly a good friend. I walk into the kitchen to retrieve my breakfast. I open the microwave door to find my breakfast. Yummy, I'm so hungry. I have sausage, eggs, grits, and sourdough toast. I'm glad he remembered what I like. I warm up the coffee, walk into the living room, plop down on the sofa, and scan the room for the cordless phone. I locate the cordless and dial Amber's number. I hear her voice on the answering machine, "You have reached the residence of Amber and Kyle Monroe, and we are unable to receive your call at this time. Please leave your name and number and we will return your call at our earliest convenience. Thank you for calling and have a blessed day". Beep. "Hi Amber, this is Syd. Call me when you get this message." Amber sounds so proper on her message, especially compared to the message on my answering machine. It's funny because I have the same message on my machine as I did when I was a teenager. At the time, I wanted to be a rapper, so I left a rap on my machine. For whatever reason, I never changed it because I thought it was funny as hell. This is what my machine says: "Hello baby, what's up with you? I'm not at home and you don't know what to do. Just leave your name and number too and at the beep I'll get back to you... baby, baby, baby." I laugh to myself because I am singing it out loud and popping my fingers. It's so funny. Every time my sister calls she reminds me that I am a grown-ass woman with nonsense on my machine. She asks me, "What if an employer calls?" I respond, "Ah hello, I'm a stripper, or excuse me, 'a female exotic dancer'. What employer is gonna call?" Then she'll go into how smart I am and how I can be doing so much better than taking off my clothes and shaking my ass in front of a bunch of strange men. "Don't knock it until you try it, and if you need to learn a few moves and tricks for that husband of yours, just let your little sis know and I'll hook you up," I holler. Amber turns her little uppity nose up and says, "No thank you, we're just fine." "I'm sure you're just fine, but sis I need you to release the beast in you. I know you have one." I laugh as she gets mad and says "I don't need to release anything, thank you and I don't want to talk about this nonsense anymore." After my good laugh, I lie back on the sofa and flip through the channels to see if I find something interesting. I drift off to sleep. I must have been really tired because I can't remember the last time I stayed at home and did absolutely nothing. I am startled by the phone ringing so I pop up to answer it. I turn to look at the clock on the wall behind me and it reads 4:30pm. "Damn, did I really sleep that long?" I look at the caller ID and its Rocky. I answered, "Hey, Rocky! "What's up baby girl?" "I must be extremely tired, because I have been sleep on the sofa all afternoon. I'm so sorry, I meant to call you to tell you to bring my babies home. He laughs, "I thought you were trying to get rid of them." "Oh no, not the case at all," I returned the laugh. "Where are you guys?" "I am leaving my sister's house." Oh Lord, he has my babies in Richmond. I hope they don't come home with fleas. "Okay, I'll be waiting for ya'll." "The boys are tired. They are in the back seat knocked out." "I guess so; hanging out with your sister and her bad-ass kids in Richmond, they will need therapy and never be the same after their visit." Rocky told me to stop talking about his family and he continues to laugh. During my much needed nap today, I dreamt about the mystery man at the club last night. I really want to see this man again. When I do, I will not let him get away without introducing myself. My thoughts are interrupted by my cell phone ringing. I grabbed the cell and look at the caller ID, it was blocked. Generally, I do not answer blocked calls, but for whatever reason I did this time. "Hello?" "Hello sexy." "*Shit*" slipped out my mouth because I knew the voice all too well. "What do you want Cameron?" He paused and says, "Syd why do you have to be so damn rude to me all the time? We use to be cool and now you treat me like a fucking step-child." "Cameron, what on earth do you want?

When I said we were through, I meant it. What part of that don't you understand? Well, sweetheart let me break it down for you. We are done. We don't hang anymore, we don't screw anymore, as much as I miss it, none of that. I don't want to have anything else to do with you because your ass is crazy and I don't need anyone like you in my life. You're not good for me, Cameron!" He yells in the receiver, "I was good for your ass for more than a year, now all of a sudden, I'm not good for you Syd? What the fuck!" "Cameron, you're controlling, possessive, manipulative, and you have a narcissistic personality. And to tell you the truth, you're like a ticking time bomb and I have no idea when you are going to explode. So that, my friend, is the reason we are no longer together." Cameron listens without interrupting during my explanation. He was so silent that I thought he had hung up the phone. "Hello, hello, are you still there?" "Yes," he whispered and then he said, "Sydney you are right, I am a ticking time bomb. I love you so much and I want us to be together. I am willing to get help for my anger issues."

"Cameron it is too late for that. I have moved on and I suggest you do the same." He yells. "I don't want to do the same!" He screams so loud into the phone that it feels as if he busted my damn eardrum. I pull the receiver away from my ear. "This is the exact PYSCHO bullshit I'm talking about. One moment you are normal then the next you're flying off the deep end. Cameron you have a serious problem and you really need help." I hear him breathing heavily into the receiver. "Cameron, I'm hanging up the phone. I'm done with this conversation." "Sydney I need you to understand that I love you, and I will do whatever it takes to make you mine again. You belong to me. We belong together." "I don't belong to anyone. Stop talking like I'm a fucking pair of shoes that you bought. You own your shoes; they belong to you, not me." As I hang up the phone I yell, "This fool has lost his everlasting mind." I look at the phone expecting it to ring. It does and sure enough, it's him. I let the call go to voicemail, turn off the ringer and grab the remote to find something interesting to watch on the tube. My head begins to pound so I make my way to the kitchen to pour myself a glass of wine. I'm in the mood for some red. The stemless red wine glasses are on the top shelf. As I reach for a glass, I think whoever thought of making a glass for different wines is a genius. I retrieve a bottle of Lombroso, an Italian red wine from Trader Joes. People are missing out on great deals at Trader Joes. Trust, they have some bomb ass wine, you can get it for little to nothing. They even have some wine, called, "two buck Chuck," their store brand for two dollars.

Chapter five

The house phone rings, it's Stanley, the doorman. "*Ms. Sydney*, you have a gentleman caller." "Okay, send him up. Please give my gentleman caller access to my floor." I know it's Rocky on his way up with the dogs. He says "Will do. Enjoy the rest of your afternoon *Ms. Sydney*." "Thanks, Stanley I will." I unlock the front door so Rocky can just enter when he arrives. I am excited to see my boys. It's been hours since Rocky took them away to give me a break. I miss them running around the house, fighting with each other, chewing on their toys, and begging for treats. The elevator dings in the distance. I patiently wait for Teddy, the big bruiser, to rush though the door with Snickers in tow, but I don't hear them coming. What I didn't expect was large hands around my neck choking me. My body wiggles as I try to turn around but the grip of the hands around my neck is too tight for me to get free. I scratch skin off the hands that grip my neck. My air supply is cut short as I fight to hang on to my last breath. I hold on for dear life. I think I'm too young to die and ask God to please save me. My eyes roll up in my head and my heart rate drops. I hear, "I told you bitch! You belong to me and if I can't have you, no motherfucker will! You understand?" Cameron tightens his grip even more, within moments I black out. Lying on the floor, Snickers and Teddy are on each side of me; licking my face and barking out of control. At that moment, I realize I'm not dead as I cough and desperately suck in air with each breath. The dogs remain by my side, barking uncontrollably. I hear the scuffling and glass breaking behind me. As I hold my throat, trying to catch my breath, I see Rocky on top of Cameron, pounding his head on the

41

hardwood floors. Cameron is not going down without a fight. Both men are throwing blows like I had never seen before. Rocky is trying to kill him! Just in the nick of time, Stanley and two San Francisco Police Officers rush though the door, one black and the other white. The black officer is short with brown hair and brown eyes and a bulky build, and the white officer is taller with blond hair and blue eyes and a more slender build. Stanley runs to me to help me up off the floor and on to the sofa.

He says in a soft concerned voice, "Oh My God, *Ms. Sydney* are you okay?" With my hands wrapped around my throat, I try to process what the hell happened. I manage to shake my head up and down, "Yes, Stanley I'm okay," I finally say in a whisper. "I will get you some water," he says. He walks into the kitchen, and opens the fridge and pulls out a bottle of water. I quickly open the bottle and begin drinking like I had not had any in years. Slowly but surely, I feel a little better but a large lump in my throat makes it hard for me to swallow. The dogs are still barking out of control and have the cop's hemmed into a corner. "Please put the dogs up," says the taller cop. Stanley and I get up from the sofa to get my dogs before they get shot. I grab Snickers and put him in the bathroom as Teddy runs over to Rocky and Cameron who are still fighting. I guess Teddy sees his buddy Rocky is in need of some K9 assistance. Stanley finally snatches Teddy up and hands him to me so I can lock him in my bedroom. The cops proceed to break up Rocky and Cameron who were fighting like two pit bulls. When pit bulls fight, they lock jaws, and it's hard as hell to pry them apart. When the cops were finally able to pull them apart, Cameron has a trail of blood dripping down his face as he screams, "I will kill your ass Rocky! You done fucked with the wrong person!" Rocky stands calm as hell, not phased by Cameron's threat, "Bring it on, you punk ass bitch. Who fucking chokes a woman? Man you're a punk ass bitch for putting your hands on Sydney. Yeah, we gonna see who's gonna get killed!" Rocky shouts. The white officer yells, "I need the both of you to shut the hell up!" Poor Stanley is in a corner with his hand over his mouth trying to gain his composure as to what is happening. He then walks over to me and places his hand on my shoulder again. "Are you sure you're okay *Ms. Sydney*? Can I get you anything else?" I place my hand on top of his and say "I am okay". "What the hell is going on here?" asks the black officer. I open my mouth to speak when Cameron shouts, "Rocky attacked me!" The black officer told Cameron to "Shut the hell up!" Then the black officer takes a second glance at him and asks, "Aren't you Cameron Wilkes, the linebacker for the Tigers?" Cameron's smug grin speaks volume as he says, "Yeah man, that's me." Unimpressed, the officer turns his head and says, "Anyway, so what happened, Miss?" That smug grin that Cameron displayed disappears. I explain to the officers that Cameron and I just broke up and he was angry. Calling me a number of times trying to apologize and asking me if we could get back together. I tell them that Cameron has anger issues and he was not taking "no" for an answer. I also explain to the officers that Cameron mentioned, "If he couldn't have me, no one could." The white officer says, "Interesting," as he looks in Cameron's direction. I indicate that I had just had a conversation with Cameron about an hour ago, I hung up the phone on him, and that was the last time I had spoke to him before he showed up to my apartment. I explain that I authorized Stanley, my door man, to let my guest up when he called to tell me a gentleman was there to see me. I was expecting Rocky not Cameron, I tell them. If I knew who really was in the lobby, he would have not been able to come up. Tears well in my eyes and I look at Cameron, "I never thought in a million years, you would try to hurt me Cameron." I manage to say. Rocky then says that when he arrived Stanley told him that he just sent a gentleman up. Rocky says, "Do you know who this gentleman is?" Stanley nods and says "It was *Ms. Sydney's* boyfriend." Rocky told Stanley he needed to get up there quickly and to call the police because, that fool is a loose cannon and he will try to hurt Sydney. Rocky continues to explain that as he entered the apartment, and saw Cameron choking me, he had to stop him which is how the fight broke out. Cameron screams, "You lying son of a bitch! I would never hurt Sydney, I love her!" The white officer looks at me, then at Cameron and asks, "If you wouldn't hurt her, then why is her neck red and her face flushed?" Cameron looks at me as tears begin to well in his eyes. I walk over to the large mirror in the entry way of the hall to examine my face and neck. "Oh My God, you crazy bastard, look what you did to me? You tried to kill me!" I charge at him, but the white officer sweeps me up with the quickness before I reach Cameron. I have no idea what I'm gonna do but I can at least try to get a good blow in. Cameron cries like a little bitch and says, "Syd I never wanted to hurt you but you left me no choice." What is wrong with this man, one moment he's saying he wouldn't hurt me then he flips and says he had no choice. "Would you like to press charges," asks the black officer. "Yes, I would." "Okay, you have to go down to the police station in order to do so," he says. I stand there and look at Cameron like he's some kind of sick pathetic human and say, "This crazy ass man just tried to kill me, so please take his ass to jail." In the next breath, the black officer says, "Mr. Wilkes, it's evident that you physically assaulted this woman; we are going to take you to the station for more questions." The white officer moves closer to Cameron and says, "Turn around and put your hands behind your back. Mr. Wilkes you are under arrest for assault." He then recites Cameron his Miranda Rights. Cameron yells, "Are you fucking kidding me? Sydney, you know I love you and I would never hurt you. I was just trying to get your attention. Why are you doing this to me?" I stare at him, "Why did you do this to me?" I shout, while pointing to my red neck. Tears well as I think how in the world I ended up with such a nut like this one. As Cameron is being escorted out of my apartment, he turns to me and with a most disturbing look on his face he says, "You will be sorry for this Sydney. Yeah, you will be very, very sorry." The look he has plastered on his face sends chills through my body all the way to my bones. I am light-headed and my legs feel like noodles. The next thing I know, I'm on the floor struggling to open my eyes. Rocky is on one side and Stanley on the other; shaking my shoulders, telling me to get up. I slowly open my eyes, WTF? As I lie on the floor trying to regain my composure, tears flow again and I begin to cry uncontrollably. I look at Rocky, "The Devil himself just told me he is going to kill me," I say. Rocky holds me in his arms and reassures me that nothing and no one will ever hurt me again, not even the Devil. I pray he's right. Stanley stands with a horrified look on his face and tears in his eyes. I can see he feels the same way, because he saw the Devil just as I did. He clears his throat says, "*Ms. Sydney* the officers said when you feel better to go down to the station to file a formal complaint and to request a restraining order against Mr. Wilkes." After about an hour or so, Rocky and Stanley leave, making sure I was okay before doing so. I lie in my bed thinking what a crazy ass day and who would have thought that Cameron would snap and actually put his hands on me. I knew I was about to take my last breath and my life flashed before my eyes. I thought about how I haven't talked to my brother and sister and I also realized that I needed to let them know that I love them every day. I thought that I was about to join my mother and father. I thought how my mother, father, and grandparents will be waiting for me in Heaven, well at least my grandparents. My mother and father will probably be in a different direction and I don't plan on going down there, if you no know what I mean. I turn on the TV and the 10:00 evening news was on and within seconds the screen flashes, Breaking News: "San Francisco Tigers linebacker, Cameron Wilkes arrested in San Francisco for domestic violence, more to come when we return." I freeze staring at the TV. I need to know how much they know, do they know it's me. I think to myself. This is going to be bad! I wait patiently for the news to come back on from the commercials and sure enough it was the main topic. The male news anchor starts to speak: "It's been confirmed that Cameron Wilkes of the San Francisco Tigers was arrested earlier today for domestic violence. We've been asked not to release the name of the victim do to the ongoing investigation. However, our sources do tell us that it is a longtime girlfriend. We will bring you more details as the story unfolds." Ten seconds later my phone rings, I look at the caller ID and its Amber. Now this heffa calls me back when she sees something on TV that concerns me, I think. I answered "Hello?" and Amber said "Oh my God! Sydney, are you okay?" I said, "Yes girl, I'm okay but that idiot tried to kill me." I went on to tell Amber all the details of what happened earlier this afternoon. I ended up in tears once again as well as Amber. She told me that she thought he was crazy when she first met him, and it was something about him that she didn't like, that he had a very controlling personality. I really didn't want to hear all that. I knew Cameron was a little controlling but who wouldn't be when you got a hot ass chick on your hip that's making mad cash shaking her ass every weekend. Amber, psycho analyzes everyone because of her profession. She's a psychologist who specializes in mental disorders, so to hear Amber tell it, everyone is crazy. I look past her comments about people being crazy because, as I said, she thinks everyone is crazy, including me for dating someone like Cameron, and choosing the career path I have. Amber is always preaching that Justin and I have so such potential, and that we could be doing so much better than we are. She keeps reminding me that we do not have to be products of our environment nor our past. Amber reminds me she still has money saved for me to go to school and get a business degree. School is just not for me, at least not now. I need money now; besides how long will it take before I get a corporate job and make an honest living? I really don't have the time to find out. I live in microwave society, and I want what I want right now. With that being said, I will continue doing what I'm doing for now until a better opportunity presents itself. After a drama-filled conversation with my sister, I finally get off the phone, and am a little pissed that I missed the update about Cameron on the news. I will just have to catch it on the 11:00pm news. I'm just not sure how this is all going to unfold with Cameron. This is crazy. How did I get here? I close my eyes and ask God to please help me get through this. Without him, I don't know how I'm going to get through this. I prayed a lot when I was a child; remembering what my grandmother told me to do. She told me, "baby whenever you are in trouble or if you need help with something just pray to God and He will help you with your problems." I guess God was really busy with other people who were in trouble because he never helped me or my sister or brother when we were younger and we always prayed... the three of us... together. I don't pray as much as I think I should. I think God is still too busy for my issues but I am going to give it a shot, and maybe He will hear my prayer and help me this time. I could really use a break. I head to the kitchen for yet another glass of wine, and then I reach for my L.A.M.B. bag to retrieve my pill container that has my Vicodin in it. I need a serious cocktail. I break the Vicodin in half, and swallow it with a swig of red wine. I'm too tired to make it to my bed so I lie back on the sofa, and cuddle up with Snickers and Teddy, looking forward to a little peace.

Chapter six

Before I know, it's Monday morning, and I need to get up and run some errands. The first thing on my list is to go down to the police station to file the report, then to the court house to get a restraining order. I want to make sure I take care of this right away with the hopes of making sure that Cameron does nothing else to hurt me. I feed the boys, take a quick shower, get dressed and make my way to take them out for a quick walk. I'm walking the boys and checking my voicemails on my cell at the same time. I must have really been knocked out because I had nine messages, and I did not hear the phone ring once. The first message was from Rocky, "Hey Syd just checking on you babe, hopefully you're getting some rest, hit me if you need me babe. I love you girl." I say out loud, "I love you too Rocky." The next message is a recording of an operator saying "I have a collect call from Justin Marshall, do you accept? Hello, hello, do you accept?" I'm upset because I missed my brother's call. The next call came from Delaney: "Sydney, it's "D" ringing to check up on you. I saw the news this morning about Cameron and I'm worried about you and wanted to make sure you were okay. Please call me to let me know you are okay." Delaney is hanging up the phone but before he disconnects, I hear him say, "That crazy SOB put his hands on my number one girl, I will"…then the phone went dead. I hit the end button and thought I will check the rest of the messages later. Teddy and Snickers handle their business and we head home. While walking back to my apartment, I notice there are two news vans; one is parked curbside at the front of my building, and the other is double parked at the parking garage. Great, what's going on now, I think. Oh Lord, please tell me the media did not find out who I am and where I live. Shit, how am I going to get pass them? I wonder. Maybe they don't know how I look or my name. They just know the address where Cameron was arrested. Yeah, that's it; they have no idea who I am. I play it cool, pass them and head towards the double doors. Stanley sees me approaching, and opens the doors. I quickly make eye contact with him and slightly shake my head; hoping he gets my signal not to say my name. He does and says, "Good morning Madame." I have one foot through the door and one of the news reporters looks up and says, "That's her." They all start for the double doors, but Stanley blocks their entrance and stands his ground. "This is private property and you are not allowed through these double doors so please step back!" he yells. I quickly make my way to the elevator and push the button. I never look back; I face the doors; praying they open soon. I hear one news reporter scream, "Sydney, are you Cameron Wilkes' girlfriend? Did he hurt you? Are you bruised? What did he do to you? How long have you two been together? How long have the two of you been having problems? Has he hit you before? Are you going to press charges?" I keep my back to them; I don't want them to see the tears rolling down my face. I ask myself again, "How did I get here?" The doors finally open and I step in not turning around. I press the button a million times believing that will make the doors close faster. They finally close and I feel a bit of relief when I make it to my apartment. I need to call somebody, anybody to be here with me. I don't want to be alone. My world is falling apart in front of me, and I have no idea what to do. I pick up my cell and dial my sister's number. She answers on the first ring and I break out into tears. She asks if I am home and I can't get a word out, but manage to say "yep." "I'm on my way Syd, just hang in there sissy, I'm on my way." I lay my head back on the sofa and close my eyes. I hear this whimpering from both dogs. I look down at them and they both have a concerned look on their faces. It amazes me how our animals know when something is wrong. I tell my baby boys that mommy will be okay, their tails wag, and then wait for the okay to hop up on the sofa. I tell them, "it's okay… come on up." They both jump up, sitting on each side of me, letting me know they both have my back. I close my eyes and wait patiently for my sister to arrive. Amber has her own key to my place, so I don't have to let her in. Within fifteen minutes, she arrives to be by my side. The dogs start to bark when she walks in which scares me. I jump up so fast that my head immediately starts spinning. Amber says, "Relax Syd, it's just me." I catch my breath and try to relax. Amber asks, if I am ready to go down to the police station to file the report. "Once we file the complaint at the station, we will need to go the court house to file the restraining order," I express. I get up from the sofa and walk into my room to get my purse and shoes. I'm dressed in a pair of True Religion Jeans, a white V-neck tee and some really cute peep toe, platform pumps. "Sydney, those shoes are so cute," Amber says. "Thanks sis, these are my newest purchase." I tell Amber that my shoes are L.A.M.B. pumps I got online and on sale, to match my bag. Amber tells me I'm such a Label Whore. I laugh and say, "Yep you're right, I am a label whore. I can't help it if I like nice stuff sis." Amber shakes her head in disagreement and says, "You can purchase nice stuff that doesn't have a name to it." I laugh again and tell her, "Everything has a name, sweetie some just have better names than others!" Amber turns to face me and says, "Girl you have issues." "Ya think, hence the reason we are on our way to the police station to file a formal domestic violence complaint." I order the boys to their crates, because Lord knows they can't have the run of the house when I'm away from home for too long. Snickers leads the way to his crate and Teddy follows. We head for the front door to start our journey.

When we walk through the front doors at the San Francisco Police Station, there are people everywhere. "Wow, there sure are a lot of people here so early in the day." We walk up to the front desk as the middle-aged, Hispanic police officer behind the desk asks if he could help us. Amber clears her throat and says, "We are here to press charges against Cameron Wilkes." The officer says, "Please have a seat and someone will be right with you." We turned to search for two seats in the waiting room. It's amazing what the police department brings in. There were a few transients sleeping in a corner, working girls that look like who did it and why. These chicks needed a bath and a makeover. They bring a whole new meaning to "stank"! We find two chairs in the back of the waiting room where we feel sort of safe from the riff-raff. We sit with our hands very close to our sides, trying not to touch anything, because I'm sure there are enough germs in this place to kill an ox. We weren't even settled in our seats when the cop behind the front desk calls, "Sydney Marshall? Is there a Sydney Marshall here?" We quickly stand and I clear my throat and said, "Yes, I'm here." The officer says, "Ms. Marshall, the detective will see you now." When we reached the double-locked doors, the officer pushes a button that makes a clicking sound, and he instructs us to pull the door open. We walk through the doors to find a very attractive young woman waiting for us on the other side. The middle-aged, African-American woman wore black pants with a black fitted shirt that accented her compact stature. She stood 5'2, and wore her jet black hair pulled back into a tight ponytail, hanging in the middle of her back. I thought to myself, how does someone this petite become a cop? How can she catch the bad guys? She did have a holster on her hip with a big 'ol gun in it, so I'm thinking, *that's* how she catches the bad guys! I laugh to myself. The detective said, "Hello ladies, my name is Candice Watson, and I am the lead detective assigned to your case. Please follow me this way." She leads us through a row of desks where there are other detectives who are busy at work. Once we arrive at her desk, we have a seat and wait for our next instructions. Detective Watson ruffles through some papers on her desk until she retrieves a clip board with a stack of papers attached to it. She then starts to look for a pen, finds one, then apologizes to us because she's generally more organized than this but it's been one hell of a morning. I tell the detective, "No worries, take your time." She finally gets settled and says, "Okay, who's Sydney Marshall?" I smile, and say, "I am." The detective skims through the report on her desk and comments that it looks like I had a rough weekend. "To say the least," I reply. She asked if I could give her my side of the story. I proceeded with the events of that day, sparing no details. As I am telling my story, the detective is taking notes. When I finished my story, she hands me some documents to complete. She then asks if I wanted to file a formal complaint and press charges against Mr. Wilkes. She informs us that if I want to file for a restraining order, I would need to do that at the court house. I respond with a very strong "Yes." The detective informs me that she could process the paperwork for the complaint. Amber and I spend about 30 more minutes with the detective, and then head for the court house to complete the rest of this process.

Before leaving the police station, Amber asked the detective what was going to happen to Cameron. The detective responds with a, "Don't worry about anything Sydney, we got this. Mr. Wilkes will be dealt with, and, if I have anything to do with it, Mr. Wilkes will never put his hands on another woman again." Amber and I look at each other, smile, and feel what the detective has said was true because she said it with so much conviction.

Chapter seven

After we finish our business, we decide to grab some lunch. I'm exhausted and ready to go home and take a well needed nap. I kiss my sister on the cheek after she pulls into the parking garage and tell her I love her and thanked her for all the support she's shown during this crazy time. Amber told me she loves me back, and heads home to get some rest as well. On the way to my apartment, I call Brandi to see if she's available to walk the dogs. Brandi's mother tells me she was still out but was expecting her any moment. She would have her come right up. As soon as I hang up the phone, it rings. I glance at the caller ID... a blocked call. I hit the end button to send the call to voicemail. Within seconds, the little phone flashed at the top of the screen; indicating I had a voicemail message. I decide to listen to the message later. I reach my floor and exit the elevator, to be greeted with an abundance of flower arrangements placed near my front door. It looks like one of those makeshift memorials when people place flowers after someone has been killed, scary thought. I wondered who in the hell sent them. I opened the door and took them in, one by one. I admired how beautiful each arrangement was once I got them inside. There were two dozen of red, pink and white roses. The aroma that came from the flowers was amazing! The other arrangements had calla lilies, lilies and other colorful flowers. I smile and search for the note card to see who was so thoughtful. I found the first note card. It read, "Baby I am so sorry, please forgive me." My smile turns into a frown. I call Stanley, to see who delivered the flowers. Stanley answers the phone on the second ring and says, "Good evening Ms. Sydney." I replied with the same greeting, and then ask who delivered the flowers. Stanley informs me they came from six different flower shops at different times. He actually thought someone had died. I was relieved that Cameron didn't deliver them himself. I let Stanley know that I have a restraining order against Mr. Wilkes and that he is not to come within five hundred feet of me. Stanley understood, and that Mr. Wilkes will never step foot on the premises again. He also said he would leave word for the other doormen. I continue to read the note cards. The other note cards read; "I love you; we belong together; no one will love you like I do; please drop the charges; we are soul mates." Cameron has completely lost his everlasting mind. I gather all the flowers, walk them down the hallway, and politely drop them down the trash chute.

It's been a long week, but I am ready to get back to work. I arrive at Club Delany's to get mentally prepared to work tonight. It's Friday night and the club is packed already…it's only 7:30. I see Delany and go over to chat with him for a second before I proceed to my private dressing room. He sees me approaching and stands to greet me. He wraps his hands around my neck and slightly kisses me on the cheek. Delany had a very concerned look on his face and stepped back just a little from his embrace to look at me. He then speaks, "Syd, how are you?" I reply, "As well as I can be." "You know you don't have to be here and you can take as much time off as you need." I smile, hug him and tell him, "I am fine" and that "working will help me keep my mind off of things." Delany tells me it's my choice and he respects it. I kiss Delany on the cheek then turn to walk towards my dressing room. In the process, I spot Rocky. He looks at me, winks and blows me a kiss. I returned the gesture. A few gentlemen try to stop me to hold a conversation, but I quickly tell them I need to head to the back to get ready for the show. I popped in to speak to DJ Mike, handing him a new mixed CD to play for my routine tonight. Mike tells me it was good to see me and he will take care of the music. I unlocked my dressing room door and walked in. I flip on the lights, drop my duffle and garment bag, and sat on the leather couch for a moment. I then open my garment bag to retrieve the four new sexy outfits I purchased. I fish around my duffle bag until I find my iPod, and placed it in the docking station on my dresser. I was in the mood for some Mary J. Blige. I scroll down until I found Ms. Mary, then clicked "all" to start the music. I turn the volume up and start singing "My Life," which was the first song that plays. I sit at the dresser and look in the mirror. I didn't apply my make-up before I left home so that it would be fresh for my show. I thought about the mystery man who had watched my every move last week and wondered if he would show up tonight. I had hoped that he did. I also thought how it might be a rough night due to everyone knowing about what happened between Cameron and me. I prayed that the incident would not have a huge impact on my cash flow. My thoughts were interrupted when I heard a faint knock on my door. I turn my music down and ask, "Who is it?" The voice on the other side of the door says, "It's Coco". I stood and walked over to open the door for Coco, who was also a fellow dancer, and really the only female at the club that I talk to. Nichole, a.k.a. Coco was a pure sweetheart and true friend. Coco enters and immediately hugs me. I thought I was about to stop breathing cause she had a nice, tight hug. "Girl, why haven't you returned my phone calls? My peeps and I were worried sick about you." "Babe it's been a rough week so please forgive me. I really had a lot going on as you can imagine." "If I didn't get in touch with your sister and Rocky, I was going to just show up at your place to make sure you were okay." I apologize to Coco again and then, shot the shit a little while longer. Coco indicates she has to bounce to get ready for her show. She performs before I do, and she was pretty good, making a decent amount of money. But there was a reason they save the best for last! Coco has three-year-old twins, a boy and a girl. The cutest little things you could ever see. She was involved with this big-time drug dealer, who is serving 47 years for a triple murder. She's doing what she needs to do for her family. I give the girl mad props for shaking her ass to keep her babies' belly full. Outside of being a dancer, she is a wonderful mother and loves those kids with all of her might. She goes to junior college during the day, and will transfer to a four-year college as soon as she can. Coco has big dreams about being a social worker to help children get out of bad situations before there is no help for them. She wants so much to help these children because she went through some stuff when she was a child, and she doesn't want to see what happened to her happen to anyone else. Again, I commend her for her goals and dreams that I know she will achieve! I return to the dresser to continue putting on my face for my performance. I turn the music back up and jam to a few more Mary J. Blige songs. I step into my first outfit for the night, a bright pink teddy with black trimming. I slide on my heels and say my prayers before showtime. I changed my intro song from "Shake What Yo Mama

Gave Ya" to "Doo Doo Brown". I was in the mood for some much needed booty shaking tonight and will pass on the slow jams for now. DJ Mike says, "Can I get everybody in this place to put their hands together for my girl, Miss Honey"... The room busts out in applause and the music cues. I open the door to my dressing room and head for the stage. Rocky is outside the door, waiting for me to make my way to the stage so he can follow behind me to protect me from the customers. I am shaking my ass as I walk towards the stage. I skim the room; looking for the mystery man, but I don't see him yet. I'm a little disappointed, because I'm hoping to meet him tonight. I make it to the stage and strike a pose to give DJ Mike the cue to move on to the next song. "Pop That Coochie" comes blasting out of the speakers and the room goes wild. I see mouths moving but can't hear anything. I stay in my zone and did just what the song said...popped my coochie! I perform a few more dances and watched man after man came up to the stage, dropping their money. Just as I was about to complete my performance, this beautiful man approaches the stage. I thought, "Hey now, well if it isn't my mystery man." He's holding a large stack of bills. I am sliding up and down the pole, when my eyes lock with his I slide down the pole and get on my knees. He lifts his hands using his index finger to make a "come here" motion. Still locked in a stare, I very seductively crawl over to this man. When I reach the edge of the stage where this yummy looking specimen was standing, I stop short when I notice he has these amazing green eyes. The mystery man gestures me to continue crawling towards him. I turn the tables and, motion the mystery man to come to the stage and stand next to the pole. I dance around him as he's watching me with great intensity. I then stop in front of him and drop it like it's hot. I bring it back up, bend over gently, rubbing my ass between his legs. I then move around him and grab the pole, allowing me to use my upper body strength. I then turn upside down, so my face is staring his package right in the eye. After my seductive dance with the mystery man, he returns to the edge of the stage. I then crawl towards him and we stare each at each other. I plant myself right in front of him; swinging my legs around in front of me, sitting on the edge of the stage with my legs on each side of him. He takes the first one hundred dollar bill from his stack, folds it in half and traces my lips, then down to my breast. He grazes my nipples with his fingers, which became hard as rocks instantaneously. He smiles, as my body responds to his touch then moves to the center of my body. He takes the bill and moves it in a circular motion near my centerpiece, not touching it, but teasing me for sure. He slides it between my legs, and then proceeds to drop hundred dollar bills like they were water. After the last bill was gone from his hand, he reached forward and slightly touches my chin, turns and walks away. Rocky was near, gathering the large amount of money. I hopped off the stage and head to my dressing room with Rocky in tow. I turn to Rocky when we entered my dressing room and said, "Who the hell is this man?" Rocky shook his head from side to side and says, "I don't know, but the brother just dropped a grip." I start to freshen up and change clothes so I can get back out there to introduce myself to him. I'm changing into a one-piece fishnet body suit. Rocky calls my name and tells me, "Babe this dude just dropped ten thousand on your ass….DAMN;

you got this brother's nose wide open!" I ask Rocky to repeat what he just said. Rocky laughs and says, "You heard me, ten thousand smack-a-roos." Rocky places the money in my safe and heads out the room. I told him I'd be out in a second. I fixed my hair, applied more lipstick, and made sure my outfit was right before I walked out. I'm going over in my head what I want to say to this man when I reach him. I hit the light, and head out to get my man. I search for my mystery man who was nowhere to be found. I was disappointed...I missed him again. I found Rocky to tell him I was gonna call it a night and need him to walk me to my car. Rocky and I exit the club and almost ran smack into a black Lincoln Town car parked at the entrance. The driver was standing next to the rear passenger door and says, "Ms. Sydney, I'm here to take you to my boss."

Chapter eight

I look at Rocky and say "what the fuck?" I then ask the driver, "Who is your boss and where would you be taking me?" The driver simply says "You will find out when you arrive." "I'm sorry dude but I'm not getting in that car and going anywhere with you!" The driver pulls out his cell phone and dials a number. He says, "One moment," into the receiver and hands me the phone. I take the phone and say, "Hello." The voice on the other end is sexy, deep and sultry. "Hello Ms. Honey." My mind is racing trying to figure out what is going on. "Who is this?" I ask. "I'm the gentleman that gave you ten thousand dollars tonight. I would like for you to meet me for a night cap, if you don't mind." "I'm sorry; I don't know you and I generally don't make it a habit of meeting strange men in the middle of the night." He slightly chuckles, "I promise I am not an ax murderer and you will be perfectly safe. My driver will give your bodyguard my name, phone number, and hotel information. Again, you will be perfectly safe," he says with confidence. I look over at Rocky who is writing the information as he glances at me and smiles. I turn my attention back to the phone call and tell the gentleman let me think about this for a minute because I was caught totally off guard. I hold the phone in my hand and wait for Rocky and the driver. I wondered who this person could be and why he just dropped ten grand in my lap and now wants to see me. I pull Rocky to the side to ask his opinion. "I've got your back if you want to roll. I know where this fool is if anything shady goes down." I put the phone back on my ear and say, "Ok, I will meet you under one condition." "I'm listening," he replies. I request we meet in a restaurant or the bar at the hotel. He agrees and tells me he wouldn't have it any other way. I hand the driver back his cell phone, and Rocky says, "Hold up, let me see the phone." Rocky pulls up the last number dialed and matches it to the one the driver gave him and he also wrote down the license plate number of the town car for extra precautions. Rocky hands the driver back the phone and looks at me and smiles. "Have fun and be careful, sis," I hand Rocky my bags, give him a hug and walk towards the car door. The driver assists me as I get inside the car and closes the door. We drive in complete silence, then finally I speak up and ask, "Excuse me sir, where are we going?" The driver looks in his rearview mirror and says, "The Fairmount San Francisco," and please call me Ben. "Thank you Ben." I lay my head back on the leather seat looking out the window and wonder what is in store for me tonight. As we approach the hotel, I get butterflies in my stomach and start to feel very nervous. I close my eyes, take in a few deep breaths and try to relax, but it doesn't seem to be working. I open my eyes to find the driver staring at me; he smiles then turns his head to focus on the road. We pull up in front of the hotel and before the car comes to a complete stop someone is opening my door. Ben quickly puts the car in park and exits the car. He comes around to my side of the car and extends his hand for me to exit the car. I give Ben my hand and he helps me out of the car. He then says, "My boss is waiting for you in the main seating area." I smile and head for the entrance. I'm approaching the entrance when Ben calls my name. I turn to find him holding my purse. I walk back towards him, "I'm sorry, I'm just a little nervous." He smiles, "No need to worry, he's a really nice guy," he says. I return the smile and walk away.

Ben then says, "By the way Ms. Sydney, I enjoyed your show tonight." I look perplexed and ask, "You watched my show?" "Yes. I've been bringing my boss to see you for quite some time now." "How long have you been watching my show?" I ask. "I'm sorry I've said too much, my boss is waiting." He holds his head down and returns to the town car. I thought to myself, this could not get any stranger. Outside of feeling nervous, I realize I have on some True Religions Jeans; a Spellman hooded sweatshirt, and some tennis shoes. Not the attire for the Fairmount Hotel. Oh well... a little late for this dilemma now. I am greeted by a very nice doorman as I enter into the hotel lobby. I slowly walk to the general seating area and see a gentleman staring at me. I walk over towards him and as I get closer; he places his drink on the table next to the chair and stands to greet me. He smiles as I approach. This man is even more attractive than when I saw him earlier. He stands 5'11, a little short for me, but I'm willing to work with that. He has beautiful caramel skin, with slight freckles on his face. His complexion is also a little light for me, but I'm also willing to work with that as well. His eyes are so captivating and a little scary at the same time. If I had to describe him, I would say he reminds me of a shorter version of Shemar Moore, with light eyes, again, not my 'BBB' Big Black, and Bald but stepping out the box might be a good thing. He extends his hand and says, "Ms. Sydney, what a pleasure it is to finally meet you." He has the softest hands I have ever felt on a man. "How do you know my name?" He points to a chair directly across from where he's sitting, and says, "Please have a seat." I did as he asks. Again I ask, "How is it that you know my name and I have yet to learn yours?"

"Well, Honey is what they call you at the club. My apologies, I'm just smitten by your beauty and forgot my manners. My name is Phoenix Davenport." I repeat in my head "Smitten by your beauty," where did this guy come from? "Phoenix Davenport, interesting name," I said. He laughs and says, "Tell me about it." I've been teased practically all my life about my name. "I've heard some worse names than Phoenix. I actually think it's kind of sexy and has a nice ring to it. Phoenix Davenport, yeah I like that," Phoenix stares at me for a brief moment then says, "Not as sexy as you." I smile as Phoenix stares at me again, this time looking through me like he was undressing me with his eyes. He finally speaks, "Yes that's right, you are the sexiest woman I have ever seen." "Come on now, you're pulling my leg," I chuckle. Phoenix has that devilish grin on his face, the same as he did the first time I saw him at the club. "Ms. Honey, I would love to pull your legs apart so I could slide right between them." Ok, now we're getting down to it, I thought. I look at Phoenix, thinking how forward he is, not wasting any time letting me know what he wants. I turn my attention back to Phoenix as he continues. "I've been thinking about making love to you for a very long time," he says. I interrupt. "Speaking of time, how long have you been watching me anyway? Does it matter?" "Yes it does." "Why?" he replies. "I would like to know if you're a stalker or not that's why." "Sweetheart, I have way too much class to be a stalker. I'm the kind of man that sees what I want and won't give up until I get it," Phoenix says with a matter of fact tone. "Oh I see," was all I could say at the moment. "I wanted to make sure the time was right before I made my move. I thought it would have been last weekend, but someone beat me to the punch with your little private dance. So I waited and felt tonight was the better night. By the way, may I call you Sydney?" I nod yes, and then ask again, "How do you know my name?" He replies, "I have my resources." I watch as a young man approaches Phoenix and asks if he wants another drink. "I'll have a Brandy please and the lady will have Malibu Rum and pineapple. Thank you," he responds. The young man walks away and Phoenix turns to look at me and notices I have a perplexed look on my face. "Is there something wrong?" he asks. I said nothing, but wondered who the hell this man really was. Phoenix says, "Sydney, I am a man who just wants to get know Ms. Sydney Marshall, that's all." Phoenix and I sit for a while, have a few more drinks and talk about each other's lives. After a few hours, I excuse myself to go to the ladies room. I feel a little tipsy as I stand, realizing I have had a little too much to drink and nothing to eat. "Oh my", I say, as I grab the back of the chair to catch my balance. Phoenix quickly stands to assist me and says jokingly, "Somebody can't hold their liquor." "I can hold my liquor just fine," as my words slur. "Maybe you can get your driver to take me home?" Phoenix looks at me and says, "Or not!" He then pulls me close to him so close that I can feel his breath on my face. His lips meet mine, keeping them there, not moving a muscle, just his lips gently touching mine. He's still, waiting to see if or how I would respond. I swallow hard, close my eyes and my heart rate is increasing, all the while, he's thinking, I got her right where I want her. Phoenix proceeds to give me the most passionate kiss I have ever experienced. He kissed me with so much depth, I literally got weak in the knees and it had nothing to do with the alcohol I had just consumed. My body was hot and on fire with passion or lust, I wasn't sure yet. All I knew is that I felt like I was running through hell with gasoline shorts on. Phoenix stops kissing me and looks deep into my eyes. I thought shit…what is this man doing to me? I ask with reservation, "or not? What is that supposed to mean? Does that mean you want me to stay with you?" Phoenix simply replies, "Yes, I wouldn't have it any other way." He grabs my hand, picks up my purse and we head for the elevator. I feel like I'm floating on a cloud. I'm not sure how my legs are moving because they still feel like noodles. Not sure what floor we landed on, but the next thing I knew I was sitting on a toilet and looking around the bathroom. The bathroom was beautiful! There was a Jacuzzi tub, a walk-in shower that looked like it could hold fifteen people, and marble floors. I felt like I was peeing forever. Finally done, I wash my hands and open the bathroom door. There was no Phoenix in sight. "Hello, Phoenix where are you?" I whispered. He said, "I'm in the kitchen." Kitchen? I thought this is a hotel room they don't have kitchens in them. I followed the slight clanking noise and found the kitchen. "WOW!" Why is there a kitchen in your hotel room? Phoenix turns to me with a spatula in his hand and says, "No, there is a kitchen in my apartment." "Okay, I know I'm a little drunk but I don't think we left the hotel," I mumble. "We didn't. I live in the hotel on the top floors where there's private living." I understand, you got it like that, I thought. He smiles and hands me a grilled cheese sandwich, "Eat this or you are going to be really sick in the morning." I thought, how sweet, he made my favorite. I ate the sandwich like it was my last meal. "That was the best sandwich I have ever had," I sang. He smiles and gives me a peck on the lips. I'm waiting for more; want more, like the kiss he gave me in the lounge. He turns off the kitchen lights and grabs my hand once again to lead me away from the kitchen. "Come with me," he says with that deep, sexy voice. Phoenix leads me down a hallway; pass the living room, the dining room, what looks like his office, and a few other rooms that had closed doors. As we approach the end of the hallway, he opens a door that leads to the master bedroom suite. I try to contain myself because it was breath taking. All I could say was "WOW!" There was a Cal King bed, to the left the master bath, and to the right a walk-in closet. There is a couch, chaise lounge, and a table in the sitting area. The walls have wood panels that separate two colors of paint and transition to amazing high voltage ceilings. Maybe breathtaking was an understatement! Phoenix says, "I have something for you", and points to the sitting area. I follow his pointed finger to find 5 gift wrapped boxes. They were all different sizes and in order according to the size of the box. I look at him and say, "Ten thousand dollars wasn't enough?" He simply replies, "NOPE." I think this is too much and I must be dreaming. Something must be wrong with this man. Oh no, I thought, he must be 'little in the middle' and that's why he needs to kick women down like this. He's over compensating, I thought. I don't care how much money you have and how many nice things you buy me. You'd better be able to put it down in the bedroom and you better have a nice package or things will not work out. Phoenix interrupts my thoughts and says, "Go ahead and open them." "You've already done so much, I'd better not." "Nonsense, these gifts were specifically purchased for you. "May I open them in the morning?" He displays the biggest smile on his face and says, "Absolutely, the best gift for me is waking up next to you in the morning." I felt it was time for me to take the lead and walk over to Phoenix, wrap my hands around his neck and proceed to kiss him. I then take his hand and lead him to the master bathroom. When we enter, again I had to contain myself. This place looks like something right out of a magazine. I walk over to the shower and turn it on. I then walk over to Phoenix and lift his shirt over his head. I admire his bare chest. There's nothing more of a turn-off than a man with "taco meat" on his chest. He doesn't have a six pack, but I can tell he works out because his body is nice and toned. I very seductively unbuckle his belt and gently slide my hands across his package to see if I can get an idea of what I'd be working with. I start to slip down his pants; he grabs my hands and stops me. Oh hell no, he is 'little in the middle' and he doesn't want me to see him with the lights on, I thought. I push his hands away and continue on my mission to get his pants down. I braced myself for the worse, but when his pants hit the floor, I was able to see a nice size bulge from his boxer briefs and was slightly relieved. I guide him to a chair in the corner of the bathroom and force him to sit. I step back and turned my back to him. I bend over while un-tying my shoe strings, which means my ass is right in his face. I slightly turn my head to see if he reacts and noticed he had a look on his face that reminded me of a pit bull in front of a meat shop, watching the butcher cut up meat. If he could salivate, he probably would. I remove my shoes and place them to the side. Slowly, I unbuckle my jeans, pulling them down exposing my dark purple G-string. I hear Phoenix say, "ump ump ump!" I stay focused, continuing with my little strip tease, removing my sweatshirt. I slowly turn to face Phoenix and find him gently stroking his package. I smile because it turns me on when a man feels comfortable to put on a show for me. I walk over to him and extend my hands to help him stand. Phoenix reaches behind me and unfastens my bra strap, exposing my perfectly round 36 D's. He lets the bra hit the floor then cups both breasts with both hands. He then turns me around and plants soft kisses behind my ears and down my neck. I moan with pleasure. He moves closer to me where I could really feel his package, and boy was I pleased. I wanted to see it, feel it, and stroke it. So I turn back around and reach to pull down his underwear. Phoenix gently pushes me back and he pulls his own underwear down. I watch with anticipation and when his underwear hit the floor, I said to myself "OMG!" Phoenix then steps up to me and removes my panties. We both step into the shower and began to caress each other. He washes every inch of my body, touching me in a way that is making me hotter than ever. I take the wash cloth and return the favor. I wash his back, his butt, his legs, and then turn him to face me. I wash his chest and move down to his package. I stroke him with such ease that he holds his head back and enjoys every moment of my touch. I get his package nice and soapy so that I can work my magic. Phoenix raises his leg and places it on the seat that was in the shower. Apparently, he's reading my mind because I really want to show him I have major skills with my hands. I stroke him and he moans with pleasure. I didn't want him to cum too quickly, so I play with him, giving him just enough to make him feel good but not to reach that point of total ecstasy. That would have to wait for later but I did want to give him a little something to get this party started. I continue to stroke him and then decide it was time to bring him to Honey land. Within minutes of gently stroking his package to more aggressive strokes, Phoenix came with so much force that he let out a loud, "Damn girl! What are you doing to me?" I smile and wash away his love juices and we both step out of the shower. He removes two cream towels that were nicely folded on the sink and dried both of us off. We exit the bathroom and head for the bed. Phoenix folds back the thick chocolate comforter to the end of the bed and fluffs up his pillows. I crawl in the bed and he wickedly follows. He pulls me into his chest and just holds me. I thought this was nice and I felt safe in his arms. Within seconds, we were fast asleep.

Chapter nine

      I wake up to the delicious smell of bacon. I turn and Phoenix was not there. I thought, wow he even gets up in the morning and makes breakfast, even though I didn't give him any. I climb out of the bed and put on a button down shirt that belongs to Phoenix. I make my way to that delicious smell. When I reach the kitchen I didn't find Phoenix, but instead a woman in her early sixties moving about in the kitchen. She was cooking and humming what sounds like a gospel song. She slightly jumps when she sees me standing there. "Oh dear, you startled me," she said. I cross my arms over my breasts because the shirt was a little see-through, and I didn't want this strange woman looking at my tatas! "I'm sorry. I didn't mean to startle you." I then ask, "Where's Phoenix?" The little woman replies, "Oh, he went out for a run and should be back any minute." I turn to go put some clothes on because I am feeling really uncomfortable. But the woman calls me back to have a seat to eat some breakfast before it gets cold. I indicate, "I should wait for Phoenix." The little woman replies, "Oh he doesn't eat breakfast honey. He will just have some juice when he returns." I sit down as I was instructed, I didn't want to be rude, and waited for my plate. The woman sat a plate in front of me with bacon, eggs, grits, hash browns and pancakes. I said "Thank you but I can't eat all of this." The woman said "Eat as much as you can. I hear you have a big day ahead of you." I wonder what she is referring to. Just then, the front door opens and in walks Phoenix, looking just as gorgeous as the night before. He walks over to me and kisses me on the lips and says good morning. I wished him good morning. "I see you met my Aunt Hattie. "Aunt Hattie then says,

"My Lord, I forgot to tell the child my name, please forgive me honey I didn't mean to be rude." I smile as I was in heaven with all the good food. Phoenix then says he was going to shower and suggested that Aunt Hattie and I get to know each other. Aunt Hattie tells me that I must be special because Phoenix never brings women home. I thought that was odd and would have to question him later about that. I didn't want to tell Aunt Hattie that this was my first time with her nephew and that I spent the night with him the first time out. So I kept my mouth closed and just listened to Aunt Hattie because she was bound to give up the info on Mr. Phoenix Davenport. I just simply said, "I guess I am." I stand to remove my plate and was surprised I ate all of my food. Aunt Hattie said "Oh no honey, I got it. You just go get ready for your fun-filled day. I ask, "Are you sure, I can really help here." Aunt Hattie said it was okay to go. I turn to leave the kitchen when Aunt Hattie said "Honey, I guess I shouldn't call you honey since that's not your name. I thought if she only knew, "My name is Sydney." Aunt Hattie wiped her hands with a hand towel she had tossed over her shoulders, hugs me and says, "Nice to meet you Sydney. Now go on and get ready."

I gently knock on the bathroom door where Phoenix was standing in front of the wall to wall mirror shaving. He had a towel wrapped around his waist and still had beads of water on his back. I ask, "May I come in?" Phoenix says "Please do." I enter the bathroom and sit on the toilet. I look up at Phoenix and say, "I have to go." I tell him that I didn't have any clean clothes and I need to take my dogs out. Phoenix sits his razor on the counter and tells me that he had all that covered. "How is that?" I question. He proceeds to explain that he called Rocky and asked if he would take care of the dogs for me and to let the club owner know that I would not be coming to work tonight. I thought; "this man has thought of everything and he also has a lot of nerve." I ask him what if I had other plans, and as he's still looking at me he says, "I apologize. I should have asked if you had any plans and not just made other plans without consulting you. But I would love for you to spend the rest of the weekend with me, if you don't mind." I tell him I would need to make some phone calls before I could commit to that. He understands and suggests I use his phone in the office if I need privacy. I tell him I will use my cell in the bedroom to make my calls. I step into the bedroom and sit on the bed. I went through my purse to locate my cell phone and had five missed calls and two messages. Scrolling down the missed calls, they were all from private or blocked numbers. I thought that could only be one person. I also thought I should get my cell number changed, but that wouldn't help if someone knew where I lived and worked. I listen to my messages and one call was from Rocky letting me know he had picked up the boys and spoke to Delaney. I thought, wow he did this without speaking to me first. I appreciated his help but would have liked to speak to him first before he called Delaney, but on the flip side, taking control like this was a major turn-on. The next message was from my sister checking on me. I deleted both messages and called Rocky. He answers on the second ring, "Hey high roller, what's up?" I said "whatever Negro! Where are my babies?" Rocky laughs and tells me they are with his niece and nephew in Richmond." Oh no! Not the ghetto kids! My poor dogs! Rocky laughs again and said they were fine, but the kids were giving Teddy a run for his money. "Ha ha, don't let my boys come home with fleas." I said. "No don't you come home with fleas miss lady," He replies. "Now you've got jokes." He said he was just kidding. "Sounds like you've got a winner. Plus he probably got the best flea treatment money can buy." Still laughing, I tell Rocky good bye and to take care of my babies. Before I hang up I ask Rocky what did Delaney say when he told him I was not coming in. He indicated Delaney said I needed more time off until all this nonsense blows over. I sit on the edge of the bed and wait for Phoenix to be done in the bathroom. When he exits the bathroom, he looks so good. This man is sexy as hell! He seems to be the sweetest man on earth. He's caring, funny, generous, and obviously very wealthy. I want to have sex with him right here and now; thinking about it makes me hot. He smiles at me and asks me what I was thinking. He walks close to me and grabs my hand to stand; he then wraps his arms around my waist and tells me how happy he is that I am with him. He tells me how he has watched my captivating performances for about four months and how everyday he thought about me, how he could make me his, how he would take care of me, how he would make me happy. I gaze into his eyes and this time I do not get hot, but I experience another feeling. A feeling I've never felt before which scares the hell out of me. I pull away. Phoenix asks me what's wrong. Still looking at him, I begin to stutter a little and managed to say, "I just remembered I don't have any clean clothes." Phoenix laughs and a calm look replaces the slight worried look on his face. "Is that it? I was worried I'd said something that offended you". "No, not at all," a lady must have clean clothes." Phoenix, still with his towel wrapped around his waist tells me I still hadn't opened my gifts and maybe now would be a good time to do so. I walk over to the other side of the bedroom where the boxes were still sitting. I turn to ask Phoenix a question and he was right on my heels. He grabs me again this time kissing me with more passion than he did the night before. I respond to his touch, his warm body, his tongue dancing passionately in my mouth. I let myself go and accepted what he was giving me. Phoenix then pulls back a little where he can see me, and says with his deep sexy voice, "I want to make love to you Sydney Marshall". Now I get hotter than I have ever been because no man has ever told me he wants to make love to me. I have been around the block a few times and have had a good number of sex partners, but not once have I experienced making love. I found myself at a loss for words, but start to un-tie the towel he had wrapped around his waist because I too wanted to make love to Phoenix. He holds my hands, which makes me stop. I'm confused because I thought this is what he wanted. He said in almost a whisper, "Not now my love, but believe me, I will have you in due time." Oh why is he playing this game, he wants me, I want him, let's just do it already! Phoenix spoke again, "I have a wonderful day planned for us and maybe if you still want me as much as I want you, we will top off the evening with making mad passionate love." I could hardly stand up because I felt weak in the knees, yet again. He held my face in his hands and asks, "Did I tell you how absolutely beautiful you are?" I said "yes, but I can always hear it again." He smiles, gently takes my chin into his hands and lifts my head so I can meet his gaze. He tells me I am beautiful and that he could easily fall deeply in love with me. He lets my chin go and turns to walk away. He stops in mid-stride, looks back at me and says "I'm getting dressed, I suggest you do the same Miss Lady," and walks into his closet. I'm still standing there like a deer in headlights and trying to compose myself. I wonder why this man has this effect on me. I'm having feelings I've never had before, remember...I don't do feelings! I love them and leave them and love is not in the sense of being in love, but more of a figure of speech...I only love Amber, Justin, Snickers, and Teddy! I turn to open the small box and Phoenix yells from the closet, "Open the big one first." The big box is sort of heavy. I am amazed by its contents once I get it opened. There are two pair of jeans; a pair of 7 by All Mankind and a pair of MEK's. There are two shirts that I assume can be worn with the jeans. There is a pair of Gucci slacks; a pair of Gucci Wedge Heels; a Fendi bag and a pair of Fendi; a very sexy black Christian Dior Evening Dress and a pair of black pointy toe Christian Louboutin Pumps. If I had to say so myself, this man really knows what I like and I was impressed. I yell, "Thank you so much but, I don't know what I did to deserve all these wonderful gifts." He sticks his head from around the closet door and said, "Because I like you!" I turned to look at the clothes and tried to decide what to put on. Surprisingly, all the clothes fit me to a "T". As I'm sliding on a pair of jeans, I say in a very low voice, "I wonder what I would get if you loved me." I was startled and almost peed on myself when I heard the voice behind me say, "Why don't you stick around and find out?" Phoenix smells good; he has on classic Levi's, a black pullover short sleeve shirt and a pair of black slide in leather shoes, not knowing the brand but I'm sure they were expensive. What he had on was simple, classy, and sexy as hell! I chose the jeans, a black semi sheer blouse and the black wedge heels. Phoenix tells me to open one more gift and then we will be on our way. I reach for the smallest box but he instructed me to open the next largest box. I open the box to find an all-black Gucci Bag with matching wallet. I turn around to thank him for yet another wonderful gift. I want to thank him another way, but that will have to wait until later. I plant a big juicy kiss on him. When I was done kissing him, he said, "You're welcome!" Phoenix and I left the bedroom and headed for the front door. The kitchen is spotless and Aunt Hattie is nowhere to be seen. I ask Phoenix if his aunt was still here. He informed me she generally blows in and out again. I thought she lived with him, but apparently she only comes over on Saturday mornings to cook breakfast when he's in town. "You travel a lot." Phoenix grabs my hand, locks the front door and we head for the elevator. When we enter the elevator he told me there would be plenty of time to learn about him. But today he wants to be all about me. I smile and said, "You don't have to tell me twice, mister and threaten me with a good time." We both laugh. We made it to the lobby and out the double doors. As soon as we stepped off the curb here comes Ben. He exits the car and opens the door for the both of us. Ben extends his hand to help me in the back seat and says good morning. I smile and enter the car. Phoenix takes his seat next to me and places his hand on my knee, caressing it for a moment. He looks at me with his hand extended, waiting for me to give him my hand. Ben looks in his mirror and asks if we were keeping the original plans, Phoenix simply says "indeed". Ben heads for our destination, and I couldn't wait to see what was in store. It was a nice day, your typical San Francisco weather, sunny but breezy. Phoenix and I were so engulfed in our conversation that I didn't realize the car had come to a stop. I look out the window and notice we are in a parking lot of some sort of port. Ben comes around to open the door and Phoenix steps out; I exit the car right behind him. "It's a little colder here by the water," I said. Ben walks around to the trunk and pulls out two jackets, "Wow you think of everything." Phoenix replies, "I try." We hold hands and head down a ramp that leads to the most beautiful boat I've ever seen. As we approach the boat I notice two gentlemen standing at the boat's entrance. We arrive at the boat and one of the men says, "Good morning Mr. Davenport," then looks at me and says "Madam." Phoenix helps me on the boat then comes on board behind me. We walk down some stairs to find a nice size sitting area. There are chairs, a bar, a table, and a restroom. The table was laced with an array of fruit. At the bar, there is an ice bucket that had some type of wine or champagne inside it and two glasses on each side. Phoenix looks at me and asks if I was ready for a little cruise. "Yes I am," I reply. "Where are we headed" I asked. "To Sausalito, have you ever been?" He asks. "No, I've lived here all my life and have never had the chance to visit." "You will love it" As the boat cruises along, Phoenix stands and moves towards the bar. He pops the bottle of champagne and pours two glasses with some orange juice. He then turns on some music and walks over to me with a glass. He hands me a glass and holds his up for a toast. I follow his lead as he says "here's to happiness". We clink our glasses and take a sip. I thought I could sure use some happiness in my life and wondered if Phoenix Davenport would be the one to give it to me. Phoenix said "Hello earth to Sydney," I turn and apologize for spacing out, he said "No worries" and asked if I cared to share my thoughts. I hesitate then said, "I was just wondering if you were the one to make me happy." Phoenix smiles and says "As I told you earlier, why don't you stick around and find out." I said to myself, I'm not going anywhere. Then said, "As I told you earlier, you don't have to tell me twice and threaten me with a good time." We both laugh again. For the next two hours, we snacked on fruit. He fed me strawberries and I fed him grapes. We laughed, cuddled, caressed each other, kissed each other and just enjoyed each other's company. When we finally made it to Sausalito; we walked hand in hand admiring the sights. I feel comfortable around Phoenix. I feel safe and wanted. It feels as though we have been together for years. For some strange reason, this feels right, it feels like we were meant to be together and this scares the shit out of me. I cannot allow my feelings to get in the way! I absolutely cannot allow myself to fall in love or at least what I think love is. Love causes too much pain and the only way I can remain in control is to not fall in love. I have never been in love, but one day I would welcome the right man that will be true to me. But for some reason I don't think he exists. However, I have only been with Phoenix for 48 hours and I feel something for him I have never experienced before. This thing with Phoenix is nice, but I can't get it twisted. He is just like the others; they only want relations and NOT relationships which is fine with me. I will ride this horse for as long as I can and remove all thoughts of feelings or love, because feelings and love do not fit into my life at this moment. Phoenix mentioned he was a little hungry and I agreed. He suggested we head back to the boat. I thought we should eat now, but I went along with the program. We make it back to the boat and it was beautiful! There were lights that trimmed the entire boat. When we entered the boat, there was this aroma that was to die for and it immediately made my stomach start to growl. The inside of the boat had been rearranged to look like a dining room. In the middle of the floor sat a table set for two. There are candles to light the room, not too bright, but just enough to set the mood. A man comes, he pulls my chair out and I sit down at the table. Phoenix follows and takes a seat across from me. He doesn't speak he just looks at me and smiles. The same man comes back with a bottle of champagne; he removes my glass from the table and pours the bubbly in my glass then does the same for Phoenix. Phoenix lifts his glass and says, "I'd like to propose a toast." I lift my glass and wait for his words. Phoenix says, "I propose a happy beginning and a happy ending." I was a little confused with his toast but imma roll with it. Our dinner is served. We're having lobster, garlic roasted potatoes, salad, and dinner rolls. And to top it off, I have this sexy ass man sitting across from me. I have no idea what's on the menu for dessert, I would only hope to be his for the night, serving it to him on a silver platter! After we enjoy our dinner, more champagne, listening to music, and cuddling on the couch, time escapes us and before we know it, we are docking back in San Francisco.

Ben is waiting as we step off the boat. He's smiling and I can only imagine what he's thinking. I'll have to ask him why he has that big smile plastered across his face later. We drive in silence in the back seat of the town car. I nuzzle under Phoenix, resting my head slightly between his shoulder and his chest. He has his arm draped around my shoulder, pulling me closer and kissing my forehead. I can smell his cologne and it's intoxicating, putting me more in the mood of having sex with him. He's quiet so I wonder if he's thinking the same. I'm in complete bliss right now, reminiscing on today's events and how wonderful he has made me feel. We make it back to his apartment and I'm looking forward to spending the night with him.

Chapter ten

I remove my shoes, sit on the couch and exhale. Phoenix is in the kitchen clicking around. He asks if I would like a glass of red or white wine. I reply, "Yes and surprise me." Phoenix joins me on the couch with a glass of red wine for us both. He rests his head on the back of the couch and lets out a deep sigh. I turn to him, rub his head and ask what's wrong. He smiles at me, touches my chin and says, "Nothing's wrong my dear, I just don't want this day to end." "Does it have to?" Phoenix smiles. "I was hoping you would say that. Will you stay with me tonight?" I tell Phoenix under one condition. He laughs and says, "Here we go with these conditions again." He waits patiently for me to give him my condition. When I didn't speak fast enough, he put his hands in the air, like he's surrendering and then says, "I'm waiting". I take a deep breath and express, "I will stay the night with you if you make love to me." Phoenix looks at me and declares, "Baby I will make love to you tonight, in the morning, the afternoon, and at night all over again, if you let me." "Well that will depend." "What will it depend on Sydney?" "It will depend on the fact that I will be able to tell the difference between having sex and making love. And I'll make you a promise; if you make love to me, and continue to be attentive to my needs...I'll never let you go! No one has ever made love to me and I want to know how that feels. I want to experience it Phoenix but I'm scared because I don't know if I can allow myself to feel love. Everyone I've tried to love or allowed to love me has ended in nothing but hurt and pain, and I have no more energy to deal with hurt and pain in my life. I have enjoyed the time we have spent together but I'm asking you to please don't play with my emotions." Phoenix stands, and pulls me up from the couch so I'm standing directly in front of him. He caresses my face with his hands which sends chills through my body. I immediately feel my centerpiece get wet and throb with anticipation. The suspense of Phoenix inside me is driving me crazy. Just with his touch I feel like I'm going to cum, right here, right now, and that has never happened! I guess there's a first time for everything and I'm willing to allow myself, for the first time, to receive whatever it is he has to offer. Phoenix smiles and replies with confidence, "Baby there's only one way to find out and I can show you better than I can tell you." "Indeed," was all I could say. Phoenix takes my hand and leads me to his bedroom. In the bedroom he picks up a remote and light jazz fills the room from the surround sound speakers that are posted in each corner of his room. He lights a candle that is sitting on his nightstand. He turns to me and kisses me with all of his might. I am experiencing something like soft lightning bolts zipping through my body. I'm completely relaxed and engulfed with fire from his kiss and touch. I feel like I'm dreaming, like this is not real and it will end soon. I hope not because I am enjoying every bit of what this man is doing to me and how he is making me feel. He starts to gently remove my clothes. I whisper, "I would like to take a shower." He shakes his head no, and says "I want you just the way you are." I succumb to his request and let him continue to remove my clothes. I start to return the favor. I smile and take him in my hands and caress his well-endowed package. I then push him lightly to the bed, look at him with lust in my eyes and the desire to pleasure him. As if he were reading my mind, he says, "Baby there will be plenty of time for you to please me. As much as I want your beautiful lips wrapped around me right now, I want this night to be all about you." "This entire weekend has been about me, why can't I take care of you for a change?" "We just had a conversation about me making love to you. I am going to do that but I want you to relax and let me do what I do. Trust me, I've been dreaming about this moment for the past 4 months, and I will let you do whatever it is you want to do with me, but not now. Do you understand?" He answered back. What could I say? How do you turn down an offer like that? I am quick sand in his hands and I shake my head "yes." Phoenix then stands, picks me up and I wrap my legs around his waist. I am in a hypnotic state when he gently lays me on the bed. I take my clothes off for a living and am comfortable with my body but for some reason, I'm embarrassed and feel the need to cover my body. I think Phoenix senses my hesitation and removes my hands from my breasts and pulls them over my head. He tells me, "Turn on your stomach, close your eyes and please try to relax." I comply. I slightly turn my head and see him reaching for the candle on the nightstand. I know this man is not about to pour that hot candle wax on me, I thought. He snickers and tells me to stop being hardheaded and close my eyes. I'm thinking he's a freak and he's going to pour hot candle wax on my back. I close my eyes tight and prepare myself for the pain I'm about to experience. I jumped when the wax hit the small of my back, my ass, and my legs, but much to my surprise; the warm liquid that was being drizzled over the backside of my body did not burn but was warm and soothing. The aroma of the candle smells amazing, and feels wonderful on my skin. I feel more heat on my back then the touch of his hands and he's now massaging my back, then ass, then legs. His touch has me in awe! I try my best to keep my eyes from rolling in my head because he is putting me in some kind of trance. It seems like I'm slipping away to another world. "Does it feel good baby," he asks. I can't speak; I shake my head "yes" and manage to moan with ecstasy. "Good! I'm here to please you." He continues to massage my body and the next thing I knew I was waking up in his arms to his light snore. I turn slightly to look at him, and he feels my movement and opens his eyes. I tell him I'm so sorry for falling asleep. He says, "Its okay you were obviously tired and needed to sleep. "It was your touch that did it for me; it took me to another place." I expressed. He laughs and says, "I'm good with my hands." "I know and so am I". I slid my hand under the covers to greet his package and he didn't resist.

I pleasured him for a few minutes with my hand but I wanted more. I want to feel him in my mouth, inside me. I roll over on top of him and start kissing his lips, his chest, and start to make my way down to his package. He moans with pleasure. "I want to make love to you right now." "Phoenix, please make love to me," I whisper. He rolls over now on top of me. He stares deeply into my eyes making me melt under him. I can feel the heat generating between our bodies when he takes his finger and is tracing my eyes, my cheeks, and my ears. He traces my lips then slides his finger in my mouth. I close my eyes and suck his finger like I would suck his dick. A deep moan escapes his mouth. He pulls his finger out of my mouth and moves down my body stopping at my breasts. He licks and sucks my nipples; they're so hard it hurts. He moves down my stomach, planting sweet kisses along the way down south. He reaches his destination and stares at my centerpiece for a brief moment. "Beautiful," he whispers. I keep 'her' nicely groomed and if you stay ready you don't have to get ready, I thought. He gently raises my legs and positions himself right between my legs. The next thing I feel almost makes me cum instantly. His warm tongue moving up, down, and in circular motions on my clit is unbearable with pleasure and it's hard for me to contain myself. I'm thinking, this is so fucking amazing, I cannot cum this quick. Phoenix is passionately kissing my clit, like he kisses my lips. A new experience, a new feeling and damn it, I love this shit. This is magical I say to myself. I can't take it anymore, my body starts to shake and Phoenix grabs my legs to keep them steady. I lift my ass off the bed and Phoenix doesn't miss a beat, he moves with me, not wanting to stop. I explode and let out a loud shout. He moans as he drinks all my love juices.

I'm captivated by this moment and my body is frozen with delight. Oh my goodness, is that the head of his dick at the entrance of my centerpiece? This man is driving me crazy. "Make love to me baby," I beg. Phoenix gently slides his dick inside me. I gasp for air and arch my back and lift my ass off the bed again; I want to feel all of this. He goes deeper, sending me into overdrive. My body's rhythm meets his and we become one. Phoenix is like a football coach, showing me all of the plays in his play book. And just like his player, I take heed to his instructions and directions. He makes my body explode multiple times. And it scares me because I have never experienced a vaginal orgasm until now. I've always had clit and g-spot, but never during the act. It was like he knew directly where to go, the forbidden zone, and once he found it, it was on. I will admit that for the first time in my life I have just made love for the very first time and it was very different than having sex. As I lay on his chest with his arms around me, vesting in the afterglow, I can hear his heart beating, and his rhythm somehow matches mine. I think about the movie How Stella Got Her Groove Back, and how Stella cried while being made love to. I'm guessing it was tears of pleasure and not pain. I didn't cry, but I wanted to because I could not believe how amazing this man was making me feel. We slept like babies, lying in each other's arms. We both are comfortable with each other, like we've known each other for years. Our bodies matched each others; we connected, as if we were meant for one another. I woke up to something that smells like French toast and bacon, and instantly thought, Aunt Hattie had returned to prepare breakfast. I slide on Phoenix's robe and head towards the kitchen. As I approach the kitchen, I hear jazz on low coming from the wall speakers and Phoenix is standing over the stove stirring something. Before I could speak, without turning around, Phoenix says, "Good morning beautiful." "Good morning." He turns around and asks did I sleep well? "Like a baby." He slightly chuckles. "Well the baby should be hungry." He then places the spoon on the side of the skillet and walks over to me, hugs me and gives me a peck on the lips. He pulls away and looks deep into my eyes and tells me, that I am amazing. I blush and said, "Well thank you. You're pretty amazing yourself!" He smiles and returns to his stirring. Phoenix prepares two plates with French toast, bacon, sausages and eggs. He sits next to me at the bar. "I thought you didn't eat breakfast?" "I generally don't, but I worked up a serious appetite last night and felt like I hadn't eaten in years." I laugh. "I can have that effect on you." Phoenix then made a comment that nearly sent me into shock. He told me that what we experienced and shared last night was so magical that he wouldn't be surprised if we created life. I damn near choked on my eggs...WHAT THE FUCK! Oh my God! How could I have been so stupid? I was so wrapped up in all that was going on that I completely forgot to use protection... I forgot to use protection with basically a complete stranger, someone that I really know nothing about! I thought I should leave immediately and rush to the pharmacy to purchase the day after pill that will at least cure one issue. I say a silent prayer, "Lord please don't let this man have any STD's let alone HIV or AIDS and please Lord, do not let me get pregnant, Amen." Phoenix sees the panic in my face and asks if I'm alright. I suddenly didn't have an appetite for breakfast anymore. I quickly stand and tell him, "This has been a wonderful weekend but I really need to go." Phoenix told me to hold on a second, and apologizes for whatever comment he made that obviously upset me. He grabs me and holds me in his arms and asks again, "Babe, what's wrong? What did I do? What did I say that upset you?" I took a deep breath and said, "Phoenix I hardly know you, yes we have spent three amazing days together, and getting to know each other. But the bottom line is I don't know you, who you are, where do you come from, who are your family, and the list goes on! We made love and didn't use any type of protection. Phoenix has this wide grin spread across his face. "This is funny to you?" "Not at all." "Then why in the hell are you smiling?" He pulls me closer and passionately kisses me. I pull back and look at him strange. He says, "I'm smiling because you said…we made love!" He then grabs my hand and leads me towards his office. He tells me to have a seat. I follow his direction. He sits behind his big oak desk and opens the top drawer. He retrieves a folder that housed some documents. He shuffled through the papers until he found what he was looking for and hands me the documents. I start to read it. The first document was a letter addressed to Phoenix from a Dr. Beckford, explaining that his last exam dated two weeks prior, resulted in a healthy exam. The documents also had blood results attached to it. I flipped through the results until I saw the words HIV Negative. A since of calm comes over my body. "Sydney, are we okay now? As you can see, I do not have any type of sexually transmitted diseases" he says calmly. I give him a half smile and say, "That only covered half of my issue." He asks, "What would be the other issue?" I hesitate for a moment. "I'm not on any type of birth control." He pushes his chair back from the desk, walks over to me and helps me to stand. Again, with that endearing stare, he says, "Babe that would not be a bad thing." Oh like hell it wouldn't, I thought. I don't have time for nobody's kid or relationship for that matter! This is crazy! Why am I having this conversation? Why am I not on my game? This man is doing something to me, clouding my judgment! Hell, I can't think straight! I done got caught up and forgot to protect myself, not only from any kind of sexually transmitted diseases, but the possibility of getting pregnant! I suddenly became sick to my stomach and rush to the bathroom. I get to the toilet just before I throw up everywhere. Phoenix is in tow, right on my heels. He enters the bathroom, wets a washcloth and holds it in his hands until I'm done. I sit on the floor and begin to cry. "Oh babe, come here." He sits on the floor with me. He leans in and wipes my face. I take the towel and cover my face. The last thing I want is for him to see me cry. He tells me to come here again and when I don't move, he moves closer to me and wraps his arms around me. He holds me for what seems like hours. He then stands and helps me up. Holding my hand, he leads me to the sitting area in his bedroom. We sit in silence for a moment, then Phoenix speaks saying, "Sydney this is much deeper than what is on the surface. Talk to me; tell me what is going on in that pretty little head of yours. Maybe I can help." I begin to cry again. I have never told anyone I was involved with about my past but for some strange reason I feel the need to talk to him. I quickly pull myself together, wipe my face and dried my tears. "One day Phoenix, but today is just not that day."

He leans in and gently kisses me on the lips, "When you are ready to talk, I will be ready to listen." "Thank you for understanding and I should be getting home. I will call a cab so you don't have to call Ben to take me." Phoenix informed me that Ben is off on Sundays and insisted that he take me home. I gather all my stuff from the weekend and tell Phoenix I had the most amazing weekend and I really don't want it to end. He threw on some True Religion jeans, a white V-neck t-shirt, and some Aldo leather flip-flops and we walked towards the front door. We ride in silence on the elevator down to the lobby. We approached the valet attendant and Phoenix asks him to retrieve his car. The attendant quickly calls someone on the phone and within seconds a white convertible Bentley appears in front of us. Phoenix pops the trunk and places my things inside, then opens the passenger side door for me to step in. He walks around to the driver's side, where the door is already open and the attendant is standing there waiting for him. He enters the car, the attendant closes the door and we drive off. Again, we ride in silence, but only for a few minutes, because shortly after we leave the hotel we pull up in front of my apartment. He reaches over and grabs my hand, once again sending shockwaves through my body. Once we park, Phoenix helps me to my apartment, carrying all my wonderful gifts that he bestowed upon me. We enter the apartment and he looks around and tells me that my place is beautiful. "Thank you. It's not yours, but it's home." "It's not mine because it's yours and it shows your beautiful personality." I thanked him again. He places my items on the dining room table and tells me that he will go so I could get some rest. I turn to face him, wanting to feel his lips against mine. I wrap my arms around his neck and stare into his eyes. His eyes meet my stare and I sense he's having the same thoughts, feeling the same tingling through his body as I'm feeling, not wanting this thing we've shared to come to an end. I move close to him and aggressively kiss him. I can feel his breathing deepen and the heat that was coming through his nostrils was turning me on even more than I already was. A moan escapes and he wraps his arms around my waist. There is so much passion between us. At that moment, my heart starts to palpitate even more all the while our lips did not part from each other's. I then drew in a deep breath and attempted to give this man the most passionate kiss he has ever had. I want to give him something to remember me by, outside of all the lovemaking we shared this weekend. I have never had a man make me feel the way Phoenix did. He studied every inch of my body, touched me in a way that made every hair stand up, tasted me, held me with so much passion and had every muscle tighten up with just his touch. It's like I had an out-of-body experience that allowed me to experience real passion and to get a glimpse of what true love could really feel like.

Chapter eleven

Okay Sydney, come back to reality I tell myself! One, because I am incapable of trust or love, and two, because I think I may have been Phoenix's weekend fantasy. I may not ever see him again. This is fine with me because we all know I don't do serious relationships. Lord knows, Cameron and I did not have a serious relationship. I push all of these thoughts out of my mind and come back into the present. I proceeded to kiss Phoenix with all my heart and soul. The moan that escapes from deep inside his throat and the feel of his manhood growing by every stroke of my tongue, lets me know that what I was doing was in fact turning Phoenix on. He draws back, looks into my eyes and takes in a deep breath, then exhales. He stares at me for a moment. I ask, "Is there something wrong?" The widest smile appears on his face and he speaks in almost a whisper. "NO, there is nothing wrong at all. I'm just enjoying you in my arms, the smell of your hair, the softness of your skin, and this uncontrollable magnetic feeling that's drawing me to you." Now a smile appears on my face. "Why, thank you mister, it's nice to know that I feel good to you and that I make you feel good." "Sweetheart you have no idea." He proceeds to tell me from the moment he walked into Delaney's and saw me on the stage, I have captivated him, intrigued him, made him constantly think about me. He knew from that moment that I needed to be his in the worst way. He wanted to give me any and everything I wanted, needed or didn't have. He wanted to make me the happiest woman in the world. He knew I enjoyed the finer things in life, material things, but wanted to give me the one thing money couldn't buy...LOVE! He knew he had a challenge ahead of him. He explains he could see a wall that stood 20 feet high in front of me, a protected bubble so to speak, that surrounds me, and knew that only true love would bring the wall down and burst the bubble that surrounded me. I stared into the eyes of this man holding on to me as if I was going to run, and think, who the hell is this man? Is this the man I've prayed for but not really knowing what I would do with him if he ever appeared? I just assumed he wouldn't for the simple fact that God never answers my prayers. He grabs my hands and leads me over to the couch. He continues telling me that even though I make so many men happy and make their fantasies come true, he wanted to know who was going to make me happy and make my fantasies come true. "When are you going to allow someone to love you and make you happy Sydney?" he whispers. I have a blank expression on my face and cannot answer his questions. "When you dance, you're in a different world. A world where there are no cares, no problems, and no love. No one can hurt you there, because you have the power and are in control of what happens. I see past the act Sydney. I see the emptiness in your eyes and the loneliness in your heart and most importantly, the hate you carry on your shoulders. I've watched you dance for months now and every time you step on the stage, I see you as an unhappy person and not because of what you do. I'm sure you enjoy that, but because of the emptiness that's inside you. This makes me want you more Sydney. I want to make you happy. I want to take you away from whatever dark place you're haunted by," he conveys. I interject, "Phoenix, I'm not sure why you think I need a Captain Save Me or a knight in shining armor, but I don't. I am quite capable of taking care of myself." I kiss him and thank him again for a wonderful weekend. He then asks when he will see me again. "Whenever you like," I reply. He tells me he would call me early in the week to arrange for us to meet. I walk him to the front door and kiss him one last time and he leaves with the biggest smile on his face. I check my home answering machine and had 29 messages. I wonder why I had so many messages. I press the play button to find out. The first 5 messages are hang ups; the next one is from my sister asking where the hell I am and why I'm not answering the damn phone, home or cell. I'd better call Amber right away… she sounds a little pissed. There are messages from Delaney, Rocky, Coco and a collect call recording from the facility where my brother is vacationing. The next messages disturb me… they were all from Cameron. Cameron left messages expressing the same things as before…how sorry he is, how much he loves and misses me, and how we needed to talk so we can work this all out. He is out of his mind! If he thinks there's even a small chance in hell that we can be together, he's sadly mistaken. I don't know why he just can't get that we are done and he really needs to get on with his miserable life. I want him to get lost and forget he ever knew me! I wonder if I should call him one last time, try and reiterate that we are done. He needs to understand I have moved on and it's in his best interest to do the same. Unfortunately, knowing Cameron, he will keep harassing me until the cows come home. I call and check in with Rocky to see how he and my boys are doing and to find out when he is bringing Snickers and Teddy home. I'm sure he is good and tired of the two of them especially Teddy, because he's a handful. I also call Delaney and catch up with what's going on at the club, I need to be brought up to speed on what drama has hit the club this week and what I need to be prepared for. Delaney is generally oblivious to what goes on with the girls; he keeps his mind on the business aspect of the club, as he should, but Coco will let me know what drama there is with the girls. I am the manager and she is my assistant manager, so we deal with these chicks, and all of their issues. I dial her number and she answers on the second ring. Caller ID is an amazing tool because she knew it was me on the other end and said, "It's about time your black ass called me back bitch," I laughed, "Well, hello to you too Ms. Coco." She proceeds to inform me that she's been trying to reach me for three days. I interrupt her and inquire about the kids. "Bitch, don't interrupt me, them brats are fine, still getting on my damn nerves." "Okay, then why the urgency to reach me?" I ask. "Does it have to be an urgent matter that I call you," she snaps back. "No, not at all but when you say you've been trying to reach me for the past three days I immediately think something is wrong." "Girl nothing is wrong just wanted to talk to my girl. Where in the hell were you anyway?" "Rocky didn't tell you." I ask? "Let's see, if he told me where the hell you were, do you think I would have been blowing up your damn phone," she snaps. I guess Coco has a point. "Where do I start?" I ask. "At the beginning bitch," she yells in my ear. Coco has one more time to call me a bitch and I'm going to let her ass have it. I hear the anticipation in her voice, so I continue with the story. Coco says, "Okay my bad, now get on with the story." "Do you remember that fine ass man that was hanging out at the club," I ask. "The one that dropped 10g's on you that night? How in

97

the hell could I forget," she replies. "Girl, his ass swept me away." Coco is screaming in my ear once again, yelling, "fuck me, girl! I want all the details and don't leave shit out!" I laugh and ask her, "How do you kiss your kids with that potty mouth?" She fires back, "The same way I will kiss your ass if you don't get to the damn story." I laugh and tell her to calm down and get ready to be blown away.

It starts with him having a town car to pick me up after I'd danced last Friday night. By the way, his name is Phoenix. Coco replied, "Cool name, keep going bitch." I snicker at her comment and continue with the story. His driver took me to meet him at the Fairmount. "Impressive, keep going," she says. I tell her to stop interrupting and listen. I continue to tell Coco about the breakfast, the boat ride, the gifts, and last but certainly not least, the amazing love making we shared. Coco is yelling again, "Girl you are shitting me! This stranger did all this shit for you? Who in the hell is this motherfucker?" she asks. I pause for a moment and say, "Damn, girl I have no idea." This makes me think again because I really don't know him. I just spent the weekend with a complete stranger and I really have no idea who he is. Damn, how did I allow myself to get caught up? I do know that he is handsome, wealthy, has a sense of humor, attentive to my needs, and he allows me to feel things I have never felt before. I hear Coco yelling in my ear, "Sydney, are you still there bitch?" Her voice brings me back from my thoughts to our conversation. "Yes, heffa I'm still here, I was just thinking about the weekend I shared with this man, and you got one more time to call me a bitch!" She laughs and says "Whatever bitch." We both bust out in laughter. "Coco you know you are a bonafide nut right?" She laughs and says, "No, what I am is someone who is trying to find some nuts to bone!" We both are laughing out of control. I tell her crazy ass I will talk to her later and end our call. Coco is crazy but I love and trust her as much as I do my sister. She has my back and I have hers and we want what's best for each other. I can talk to Coco about any and everything without her judging me. She and I are so much alike. She's been through just about as much as I have and knows my pain. We've shared so many deep conversations, discussing our deepest darkest secrets. I lean back on my sofa then decide to move down to the left side of the sofa to the chaise section, giving myself time to lay back and relax. As soon as my head touches the pillow on the back of the chaise my mind suddenly drifts back to the events of the weekend with Mr. Phoenix Davenport. Although I had a wonderful time with him, I'm very upset because I got caught up; I let my guard down and allowed him to enter some place that no one has entered before...my heart. Phoenix and I clicked and connected on all accounts and it was like we have known each other for years. As a golden rule, when I get involved with someone, so to speak, after we've screwed, I bounce. This way there's no emotions and no confusion. I don't need to cuddle, spend the night or have breakfast in the morning. Even though, Cameron and I spent a lot of time together, it was different. I wanted to spend quality time with him, going to the movies, romantic dinners, walks in the park, but that was not the kind of relationship we had. I was the trophy girl for him. He showered me with gifts, trips, fucked me right but most importantly being on his arm was all a part of my plan to stay in the lime light and get the exposure I needed to get ahead in the business. Let's keep it real, we all know it's not what you know but who you know. Hanging with Cameron put me in contact with so many people that helped me fill my pockets as fat as I wanted them. So, I guess his crazy ass was good for something but I knew deep down inside he was foolish on and off the field. I was able to control Cameron and deal with his personality because I knew we could never have anything serious other than what we had, a bunch of fun. Phoenix on the other hand, did something to me; he made me not want to leave his presence. I wanted to be wrapped in his arms forever; I was hooked on Phoenix! I guess you can say my nose is wide open. This is an unfamiliar feeling for me, but I like it. All I can think about is his touch, and how his touch makes me feel. I had to inhale, I felt as if I were losing my breath. His touch is so smooth and soft that my body heats up and my centerpiece tingles just thinking about him. I want to melt every time I'm in his arms. No man has ever made me feel this way and the fact that he expressed how he wants to be with me, love me, take care of me, and be the man he knows I need, is deep and scary! I'm scared mainly because men always want something from you. They can't just love you or take care of you without some type of motive. I ask myself, what does Phoenix Davenport want from me? I have a hard time trusting any man, that's why I need to guard my heart, don't let them in and they won't hurt you. I don't do the whole love thing because it keeps me safe and out of harm's way. My thoughts are all across the board. I had an amazing time with Phoenix and he is like no other I've been with which makes me think he could possibly be the one I give my heart to. I sit on the chaise for a few more moments with my eyes closed and this little voice inside my head tells me to shake this shit off, you had a wonderful weekend, but remember you don't do love and every man that has come into your life has hurt you and will hurt you! So, in order to guard your heart you will need to let him go before it's too late! My thoughts are interrupted by my cell phone ringing. Still with my eyes closed, I reach to the right and grab my cell phone and click the talk button. I answer "hello" and the voice on the other end sends chills my down my spine but not the chills I experienced with Phoenix this weekend, these are chills of the worst kind. Cameron's voice came through the phone deep and raspy, "Hello Sydney my queen." "What do you want Cameron, why are you calling me?" There is a slight irritation in his voice. He tells me I know what he wants and it's me and he will not stop until he gets me back. I sigh and tell Cameron no one gives a shit about what he wants, and his wants are one-sided and he needs to get a fucking life! I explain to Cameron that he is in a bad place and needs to get some help. I tell him that with time maybe we can be friends but as far as us being together, it's not going to happen. OMG why in the world did I say that? Cameron starts screaming in the phone so loud that I have to move it away from my ear before he bursts my eardrum. "I don't want to be your fucking friend; I'm your fucking man!" He proceeds to tell me that I am his and no one else can have me, what does he need to do to make it right, to get me back? Cameron tells me that he loves me like he has never loved anyone else and it's killing him that we are not together. He sounds like a broken record, and I've heard this all before, blah, blah, blah! I interrupt

Cameron with laughter and politely tell him that it's funny that all the time we were together never once did he tell me, express to me, or show me that he loved me. "Cameron, I was only some good pussy to you, someone who looked good on your shoulder. That's not love Cameron. Love is when you kiss someone and their bodies melt together and become one. Love is spending quality time, out of the lime light, getting to know each other, their wants and desires, knowing their deepest darkest secrets and thoughts. Love is knowing that the person you are sharing your bed with has your back no matter what, and is your best friend in time of need, knowing when to not speak and just listen, will go to the ends of the earth for you, will die for you. That's what love is Cameron and believe me, you have none of these qualities I've just described." I explain to Cameron that the only things he loves are: money, football, pussy, and himself and in no particular order, which makes you incapable of love or loving anyone. It was silent on the end but I could hear him breathing. I continue and tell Cameron he's a cool person to hang out and party with but as far as us, it's a done deal! "Cameron, I'm sure there are plenty of chicks out there who are standing in line to get with you." He didn't respond to my comment. For a moment I thought I heard him crying then he finally spoke and tells me that he loves me more than I'll ever know. He asks me "Don't you feel the same about me?" Okay, this nut has truly lost it, has he not heard what I've said for the last 20 minutes we've been on the phone! To answer your question Cameron, "NO, I don't! We had fun hanging out together. Why do you think I never got upset about the rumors of you with other women, you know why, because I didn't care who your flavor of the week was. I knew I was your main chick and there were plenty of you to go around and you had no problem spreading yourself with as many women as you could. So do me a favor boo, after all we've been through, it's really time to go our separate ways. I can't say it any other way." Again silence. He tells me he loves me and the pussy and that if he can't have me then no one can! "First of all, the last time I checked, the pussy you are referring to is on my body which makes it mine and I decide who to give it to! Second, are you threatening me Cameron? Do I need to remind you of the restraining order? I'm sure you don't want to go to jail again, or worse, get kicked off the team for domestic violence. I need you to think long and hard about all that you stand to lose, if you continue on this path." He laughs this wicked laugh and replies, "I'm not threatening you at all babe, I'm promising you"…then the phone went dead. When he made that comment I got the same ire feeling I did when he was being arrested in my apartment for choking me and my gut tells me this me this is not over. I close my eyes and pray that God protects me from the maniac. I keep my eyes closed for what seems like a few minutes, but I drift off to sleep.

Chapter twelve

I jump as my cell phone rings and breaks me out of a slight slumber. I open my eyes and reach for my phone. I look at the caller ID this time not wanting another draining conversation with Cameron and the screen indicates that it's a private number. I hesitate but answer anyway thinking if it's Cameron again I will just hang the phone up. To my surprise the deep sultry voice on the other end was speaking in what sounds like French, Phoenix proceeds to say:

"Bonne soiree magnifique, je ne peux pas m'empecher de penser a vous.

Vous avez ete dans mon espit a partir du moment j ai quitte cet apresmidr.

Mon corps et mon spirit que vous implore et j ai besoin d'etre pres de

chez vous, vous vous sentez, vous sentez une odeur,

et faire l'amour avec vous".

"As sexy as this sounds Phoenix, I have no idea what you just said." I tell him. Phoenix laughs and begins to speak to me in English:

"Good evening beautiful, I can't stop thinking about you.

You have been on my mind from the moment I left you this afternoon.

My body and mind craves you and I need to be near you,

feel you, smell you, and make love to you".

It doesn't matter what language he speaks to me, I have a smile on my face from ear to ear. He's making my "centerpiece" moist and I'm getting hotter than someone running through hell with gasoline briefs on. Phoenix calls my name as he is still talking to me, I must have zoned out because he's calling my name: I am speechless and respond, "Yes, I'm still here." I tell Phoenix what he just said to me was so sexy and it has me hot. He chuckles and says he can recite what he said in four additional languages. This man never ceases to amaze me and I'm impressed. "Maybe one day I'll get to hear those other languages," I reply. His voice sends chills through my body. He tells me that he knows we just left each other's company earlier today but he needs to be near me. Still smiling, I ask, "What are you waiting for?" "An invitation," he sings. The next voice I hear is Stanley asking is it okay to give access to Mr. Davenport. "Yes, Stanley, please let Mr. Davenport up." I didn't expect him to be downstairs; I haven't done a thing with myself since I saw him earlier. My duffle bag is still in the middle of the floor, my shoes are kicked up under the coffee table in the living room and I look a HOT mess! Before I know it I hear the chime from the elevator ring out in the background and seconds later, my door bell rings. I briefly stop at the mirror in the hallway on the way to answer the door to straighten my hair a little bit. I remove my ponytail holder and place it on the half-moon oak cherry table right under the matching mirror. I run my hands through my hair allowing all the loose strands to fall back into place. I place the ponytail holder back in its place in the middle of my head; I turn to the side one last time and look in the mirror before the doorbell rings again. I yell, "Hold on mister, keep your draws, on I'm coming." He laughs and says, "That's hard to do when I'm this close to you." Wow, he really knows what to say to make a girl feel good. I make my way to the door and when I unlock the top and the bottom lock, the door opens to the most gorgeous man standing in front of me smiling with the straightest, white teeth I have ever seen, holding bags in his arms. He holds up the bag and says, "I've come baring libations and vittles". "Well come on in with your bags Mister. You brought food, how did you know I was home?" "I didn't; wishful thinking I guess. I wanted to be ready in the event you were available," he states.

He walks in my apartment, comfortable and heads to the kitchen. He places the bags on the kitchen counter, and then walks over to the living room, sitting on the sofa. I follow suit and sit beside him. He places a bottle of wine on the coffee table and grabs my face with both of his hands. He plants soft kisses on my chin, on my nose, my forehead and my cheeks. He reaches my lips, then stops, not kissing me. I can feel him breathing, feel his breath come out of his nose and the warmth hits my upper lip, the anticipation is killing me. Kiss me already! I say to myself. This man is doing it to me again, making me hotter than ever. I'm burning with desire and he is driving me crazy. Without touching me, my breathing gets heavy and I can barely control my impulse to take his lips into mine and allow our tongues to do the tango. I look at him and he has this devilish smirk on his face like he knows exactly what he's doing to me. I know deep inside this thing we have is not just physical, it's more than that. I can't really explain it, but there is a connection that is undeniably magnetic. I guess he figures he's teased me enough because without warning he aggressively enters my mouth allowing his tongue to swim around in my mouth which made me moan with pleasure. After a few more minutes of passionate kissing he pulls away from me and slightly steps back and lifts my shirt over my head exposing my erect nipples. Phoenix removes my bra and proceeds to devour my nipples moving from one to the other, capturing both of them not wanting to show more attention to one than the other. He takes his hands and moves them down my waist until he reaches my pants. With one hand, he skillfully unbuttons my pants and I step out of them. He slides his hand inside my panties and with his finger he massages my love button. I moan with pleasure! When he slides his finger inside me and feels how wet I am, he looks up at me and says "Did I do that?" in his best impression of Steve Urkel. "You most certainly did." Phoenix has some serious skills. With his finger inside me, he stands up and whispers in my ear, "There are so many other things I want to do to you Sydney Marshall". I manage to open my mouth and force the words out, "Please do with me whatever you want." "Good, step out of your panties." I obey his command and come out of my panties. He slides his hands under my arms and lifts me up where my lips are directly in front of his. He starts to kiss me again as I wrap my legs tight around his waist. While kissing me, he backs up and we're both leaning against the wall. I feel the coolness of the wall as my bare back touches it which makes me arch my back, but the heat that is generating from this activity quickly takes the coldness away and I let out another moan. Phoenix doesn't miss a beat, as he moves through the living room carrying me. As I lean up against the wall, he removes his hands from around my waist and moves them to my legs. He grips my legs and lifts me so that I sit on his shoulders where our lips meet...again. This time my centerpiece lips make contact with his mouth. I feel his warm tongue brush against my clit and it damn near drives me insane. He moans out load as my juices are flowing like Niagara Falls, faster than he can handle it, so I thought. I feel my body start to quiver, Phoenix is working his tongue and I am about to cum. I hear him moan again as he knows the moment is near. I'm holding back because I don't want it to end, I want him to keep doing what he's doing but I can't control myself and I explode, letting out a loud scream of ecstasy that even scares me. He continues to drive me crazy and I am begging him to stop because I can't take anymore. He finally hears my plea and stops but not before looking up at me to tell me that I have the sweetest juice he has ever tasted. All I can do is smile. Phoenix gently slides me down the wall and plants my feet on solid ground, he takes my hand and leads me to my bedroom. My body shakes from aftershocks of the fantastic orgasm I just experienced. We enter my bedroom and he gently lays me on the bed and lies on top of me kissing me passionately. I aggressively try to roll him over and my first attempt fails. I take a deep breath and try again, this time I succeed and he was now under me. "You always have to be in control, don't you?" I place my index finger on his lips and said, "Shhh, yes I do!" I then proceed to remove his shoes, pants, shirt, and then his underwear...exposing his rock hard package. My mouth starts to salivate as I look at him. His package looks like an extra-large big stick on a hot summer's day and all I want to do is suck it until it melts in my mouth. He tells me that I need to learn how to let someone totally and completely take care of me and I need to stop putting up this defense all the time. I tell him to be quiet and let me work my magic. I start by licking his legs, caressing them, then make my way up to his manhood and grab it like it's a snake out of control. I gently place soft kisses on the tip, he moans with pleasure and I think to myself "oh boo you haven't felt nothing yet." I reach in between my mattress right below where I was lying to get some added pleasure all while still stroking him, I glance up at Phoenix and he is in total bliss. I retrieve my 10-speed clit bullet. Its main function is for clitoral stimulation but tonight I will be using it for added pleasure when I'm pleasuring my man with a hand job and blow job. Anyway, I turn the bullet on the first speed because I don't want to scare the hell out of Phoenix, so I decide to take it slow. I replace my hand with my mouth and Phoenix immediately arches his back. It's nice to know that my skills are driving this man crazy. As I'm moving my mouth on and off and all around his manhood, circling my tongue around the head of his penis, he's moaning and this is the perfect time for me to add to my performance. I gently place the bullet on my cheek as I have him in my mouth so he can feel the vibration. This drives Phoenix wild, he never looks up to see what I have added to our oral play, he just shouts, "Oh shit woman, what are you doing to me?" I reply, "The same thing you do to me, give you absolute pleasure!" "Indeed," was his response. "You should be called Trixie instead of Honey, since you pulling out tricks and all." "Then Trixie I'll be!" I laugh. I continue to bring Phoenix to pure ecstasy when I feel him growing even larger in my mouth, I remove the bullet from my cheek and place it under his balls, and this man has no idea what hit him! His body starts to shake, and he explodes in what may have been a 7.0 earthquake. Phoenix is speechless and is unable to move for several minutes. I crawl in the bed to lie next to him, he looks deep into my eyes, kisses me on the lips then on my forehead. He wraps his arm around me to draw me closer. He lets out a deep sigh, whispers in my ear, "I'm falling in love with you Sydney Marshall, not because the sex is amazing but because you are amazing!" I have the biggest smile on my face, and then chills run through my body. All of a sudden, I'm consumed with fear, because I think I feel the same! Am I able to love? I question myself. Within seconds our bodies mesh together as we lay and become one. The beats of our hearts seem to be in synch with one another and I feel completely safe in this man's arms. What's happening to me? I ask myself, why do I find myself sometimes thinking about him all day long? I cannot fall for Phoenix Davenport...or is it too late because I am feeling something I have never felt before in my life. We must have worn each other out because I slept like a baby. I woke up to a note on the pillow next to me that reads:

My love, you were sleeping so peacefully I didn't want to wake you. I have an early meeting conference call and will call you a little later when I think you are up and about. Until then my love.....hugs and kisses!

BTW, I hope I can concentrate in my meeting today because you got me all messed up with that little number you pulled on me last night!

If you like, come by the apartment, I'll be working but would love to have you there. No need to call, just come.

I smile knowing that I made Phoenix happy. I lay in the bed for a few more minutes before I get up to shower and get ready to meet Rocky for breakfast and swoop up my doggies. Rocky tells me he is happy to see me and he was about to call the Calvary to come find me since I was missing in action for a few days. He's so damn silly. We talk about how something's going on with Delaney and that he wants to talk to me about the business and some changes he wants to make with the club. Rocky seems to think that Delaney might be sick or something because he has been acting different lately and that he needs a break from the club for a while.

I'm concerned because I need to know what's going on with the boss and its obvious Rocky does not know all the details. Delaney can be very private but I know how to get it out of him without any effort on my part. I make a mental note to call him this evening to find out what the deal is. I continue my conversation with Rocky about my weekend with Phoenix and how he really seems to be a different guy, how he is so different than any guy I have been with. I tell Rocky that I know I have not known Phoenix long but he brings out feelings in me that I didn't know I had and that it scares me. I express to Rocky that I think I'm falling for this guy. Rocky has a disappointing look on his face that lets me know he is not happy with what I just said. I ask him, "Why are you looking at me like that?" He stares at me for a few more minutes and again I ask, "Why are you looking at me like that?"

Rocky shakes his head and says "No reason". "There has to be a reason for you to look at me the way you did." He hesitates for a second, "Syd, you know I love you and don't want to see you get hurt." I chuckle, "Babe, I love you too and you know me, I'm a tough cookie. I can handle myself and trust I'm not going to get hurt." "What do you know about this guy Syd?" I think for a second and respond, "Enough. What I do know is that he is kind, loving, attentive to my needs, he cares for me and he is rich! This is nice to have all that rolled up into one nice package wouldn't you agree?" I respond. Rocky still has a perplexed look on his face. "Sydney, I'm not rich but you know I care for you. I'm kind, attentive to your needs, and loving as well." I smile and wonder why he is telling me this. "Yes, I know you do babe, you're my 'rock' but it's different with you." At this point Rocky appears to be irritated and says sarcastically and in an escalated tone, "*IS IT*?" His question shocks me and I think, "Where in the hell is this coming from? Rocky, we have known each other for a long time; you are my brother's best friend and I look to you as a brother. You're my brother from another mother. So I'm a little confused by your statement. I'm not sure where this is coming from. Is there something you want to tell me?" His response was dry and distant, repeating what I said, "Yeah, a brother from another mother." I detect sarcasm in his voice and I decide to dismiss his attitude and will address it at a later time. We catch up for about an hour or so more then he tells me he will use his key and drop the dogs off later. After leaving Rocky, I decide to stop by Phoenix's for a second before I run some errands. On my way to Phoenix, I think to myself I need to do some investigating to find out as much as I can about Mr. Phoenix Davenport because even though I like what's on the outside and I enjoy his company, I still need to know more. I make it to his apartment in no time and leave my car at the valet and head to the elevator. I press the penthouse button and ride up with butterflies in my stomach. As comfortable as I am with him, he still makes butterflies flutter in my stomach. I reach his floor and step off the elevator, straighten my clothes and run my tongue across my teeth to make sure I have no food in them. I ring the doorbell and in seconds Phoenix answers the door. He's so handsome in his sweat pants and no shirt. He has a headset on and is talking in the speaker attached to his ear. He motions for me to come in. I enter the apartment and walk to the living room to take a seat. He pulls me up and holds my hand while leading me to his office. Once in his office I sit on the couch and he moves to his big oak desk, still participating on the conference call. He puts his finger up to his month, indicating he wants me to be quiet. I obey. He then removes the headset from his ear and places the call on speaker. I'm sitting on the leather couch watching him and thinking he's so damn sexy. As he is conversing with others on the call, he walks over to me on the coach, bends over and kisses me. He grabs my hand and we walk over to his desk. He picks me up and sits me on the desk and kisses me again. He then sits in his high-back leather chair and answers a question someone asks him on the call. While he is sitting in his chair, he's staring and smiling at me. He then stands, lifts my legs, and pushes my shirt up over my hips. I start to speak, and he put his finger up to his lips, telling me to be quiet. I obey. He then unbuttons his pants, letting them drop to the floor. He moves my panties to the side and runs his finger over my 'centerpiece' raising my body temperature 100 degrees. He responds to another comment on the call… this shit is turning me on. I look down and he is hard as a rock and his manhood is pointing in my direction. I smile. Phoenix moves closer and I lay back and let him have his way with me. He enters me and it's hard for me not to gasp. I keep my composure while he makes love to me while still on the conference call. This man has mad skills and what he's doing to me is super sexy. I am completely taken aback. Someone asks him did he agree with the last statement, and he shouts, "Oh yes, that was good," as he came at the same time. The man on the other end replies, "I'm glad you're so enthusiastic Phoenix," "Indeed." I get myself together, kiss Phoenix and write on a piece of paper that I will talk/see him later. He kisses me and I head for the door. I am all smiles. I can't believe what just happened. Wow is all I can say. I check my voicemail and Rocky has left me a message with a change of plans. He dropped the boys off at the groomer's and needs me to pick them up. "No problem, it's on the way home," I say out loud. I can't get this smile off my face, I am so happy I can hardly handle my happiness. I make it to the groomer's and retrieve my boys. They're exhausted and hop in the back seat and are sleeping before I pull away from the curb. Looking in my rearview mirror, I notice a car following me as I drive home. I need to stop tripping and being paranoid, nobody is following me, I said to myself. As I approach my building, I notice the car following me looks like the same car that followed Ben and I the other day. I pull up to the garage gate and the car parks at the entrance again. I look to see if I can see anyone in the car or behind the wheel but the windows are so dark I can't see anyone. I think to myself, there are a million cars like this in the city, so why am I tripping. I hit the remote to open the gate to enter the garage and as I start to pull in the carport, the parked car then burns rubber and pulls off quickly. I hit the brakes and look in my rearview mirror to see what's going on and all I see is the car pulling off leaving a faint trail of smoke behind it.

Chapter thirteen

Okay, now I'm spooked because whoever is in that car was apparently following me and this time I don't think it's a coincidence. I pull into the garage and pull into my designated parking spot. I sit for a second to gather my thoughts and try to calm down. I retrieve my cell phone from my purse to dial Rocky's number but I don't get much service in the underground parking garage. I observe my surroundings before exiting my car. I open my door and close it, then open the passenger side door, pull the seat up to get the boys out the back seat who both were sleep and didn't have a clue as to what just happened, not that they would anyway...I have to remember they are dogs not humans, well they are like four-legged humans to me. I grab their leashes and lead them out of the car, close the door and hit the alarm and we proceed to the elevator. As the elevator door opens I hit the main floor button. The door opens and the boys run out to greet Stanley. He smiles, kneels down and they run directly into his arms and licks him in the face. Stanley is happy to see them and plays with them while I collect my mail from the mailbox. Stanley stands and says, "Ms. Sydney I'm glad you stopped by I have flowers for you." I smile at Stanley and tell him, "Oh you shouldn't have." He returns the smile and says, "I didn't." He tells me they were delivered about an hour ago and there was no card attached. A wide smile appears on my face and I instantly think that Phoenix was behind this. I ask Stanley if he noticed the black car with dark tented windows parked outside. He looks concerned but responds, "No." I tell him okay and walk towards the elevator calling the boys behind me. As the elevator door opens, I step in and the boys follow right behind me. I make it in the apartment and get the boys settled. I gave them some fresh food and water and then I grabbed me a glass of wine. I plop down on the sofa and search for the remote to turn the TV on. I click the switch and surf the channels until I find a Criminal Minds marathon. I retrieve my cell phone again from my purse to call Rocky. He answers on the second ring and I can still hear an irritation in his voice. I tell him about the events of this mysterious black car with the dark tinted windows. By the time I finish running it all down to him from the night in the club parking lot, to the hotel entrance, to today's event, he is really pissed off because I was just now telling him about the situation. His voice has raised an octave as he is yelling now, "Why the hell didn't you tell me all of this earlier when we were together?" I tell him to calm down and stop yelling at me. He quickly apologizes and indicates how important stuff like this is and can't be withheld. I tell Rocky that I really didn't put two and two together until now. "I have no idea who it could be." He suggests that it could be a number of people because I have 'fans' as he calls them when in fact they are stalkers. He offers to come over to make sure I am okay because he's here to take care of and protect me. "I'm fine. I feel safe and secure in the comfort of my home and I will be in for the evening." He gives me specific instructions not to leave the house without contacting him first so he can come over to make sure I am okay and to take me anywhere I need to go. I laugh and tell him, "You act like I'm a celebrity or something. I'll be fine; I don't need a full time body guard." He informs me that I will have one until we get to the bottom of who's following me and until it's taken care of. I agree, to get him off the phone. I grab the glass of wine off the coffee table and take a long sip, savoring the taste of the red wine that is swimming around in my mouth. I get up and head to my room to get my laptop. I retrieve my laptop and head back to the sofa. Approaching the sofa, my cell phone rings and I reach down to answer it. The screen displays that it's a blocked call; I click the end button to send the call to voicemail. I'm not in the mood to deal with any nonsense tonight. I sit down and open my laptop and power it on. When it finally comes on I go to the internet explorer and log onto the web. The Google search engine appears and I type 'Phoenix Davenport' in the box and hit search. Much to my surprise as soon as I clicked search, there appears Phoenix's name. I'm sure there are not a million people with this name but there are several articles listed under the search so I start with the first article and will work my way down. This article caught my undivided attention. It was in fact my Phoenix because his photo appeared with the article. I begin to read the article and I am in a state of shock. The article indicates that Phoenix is the 25th richest man in the US. "What the fuck!" comes out of my mouth...I continue to read and find out that he is the co-founder, CEO/President of a company that manufactures, builds, and sales luxury cruise liners. My mouth is on the ground and I am still in a state of shock. I read how his father was the founder of the company and when his parents passed away, the business was left to Phoenix and his twin sister. That's interesting, Phoenix never mentioned a sister, let alone a twin sister, I thought. His father was an only child and his mother had one sister 'Auntie Hattie' who had no children and declined to help him run the company. The article indicates that Phoenix and his twin sister were groomed to take over the company and by the time they graduated from Oxford, in England they came on board right out of college, Phoenix as Vice President of International Affairs and his sister as Vice President of Marketing. They both were naturals and settled into their positions as expected. Unfortunately, his parents and his sister were unexpectedly killed in a car accident by a drunk driver. I am in shock; I had no idea that he lost his mother, father and sister to a drunk driver. "Why me? Why did he seek me out?" I ask out loud. I am clearly from the wrong side of the tracks, but he sought me out, without me knowing who he was. I then think that Phoenix and I have a lot in common, we both lost our parents, however, I was young and raised by my sister and he was older and left to run a multi-billion dollar company. There's no doubt he was born with a silver spoon, and I was not but we share a lot in common. "Why is he attracted to me? What is it he sees in me? Why me and not some highly educated woman who is his social equal?" These are questions I'm asking myself. I've been involved with many men who have plenty of money but none of them compare to the résumé Phoenix possesses. I'm really apprehensive now because I am obviously way out of his league and social status. I quickly snap out of having a slight pity party and remind myself that he approached me, he was the one who came to the club for several months to see me; it was not the other way around. I have nothing to offer this man except a banging body, beautiful looks, personality plus, and according to him 'the best lover' he has ever had. I guess that's worth millions! I lay my head back on the sofa and think can I really fall in love with this man? "NO," I say out loud because I don't do love, I remind myself. The feelings I have for Phoenix are genuine, I was falling for him prior to knowing he is one of the richest men in the US. Looks like he was searching for gold, better yet a diamond in the rough, but in his search, he got me. A huge smile appears on my face and I think back to him telling me, he wants me for who I am and just the way I am. That makes me feel good because he knows I don't match his social status but that doesn't faze him because he knew what he was getting from the start and that didn't stop him from getting what he wanted! Another reason I know I'm falling for him is because believe it or not it was not just about the sex or the material things he gave me. It was about the way he held me, touched me, kissed me, talked to me, that let me know he's different and that he wants me for me and all that comes with that. My mind is racing a million miles an hour and I am struggling with the two voices in my head, the one that says, "Run for the hills before your heart gets broken," and the other that says, "You deserve love and to be happy, let down the wall and allow yourself to fall in love for the first time." I finish my wine and the boys and I head to the bedroom for some much needed rest. I settle in the bed and before I close my eyes, I pray:

"God, you know I have major issues and that I have been through a lot in my life. You know I have a wall protecting my heart because as you know I can't trust men because they always hurt me! Me and love just don't mix, so I pray that if Phoenix Davenport is in fact that man I will fall in love with and that will not break my heart as every man in my life has, please show me a sign because I don't want to second-guess

all the feelings I have stirring inside me. I know I don't pray as much as I should but deep down inside I desire to be in love with a man who will love me for me and not hurt me. I think I deserve it, no God, I know I deserve it, so I ask that You answer my prayer. God please make it plain so I will know that Phoenix is the one or if he's not for me then by all means give me a sign as plain as a billboard that reads " he's not the one" and I will run for my life as if I am being chased by a grizzly bear. Thank you God for listening to my prayer, AMEN!

Before I close my eyes for the night I want to hear Phoenix's voice. I pick up my cell from the nightstand to dial his cell number, Phoenix answers on the second ring. I greet him with a sweet and warm, "Hey you." "Hey yourself. I was just thinking about you," he replies in that deep sexy baritone voice. He says he is in the middle of a meeting and asks if he can call me back. I glance over at the alarm clock on the nightstand and it reads 11:37 pm. "Someone's burning the midnight oil." He laughs and says, "I will once I get to you." I hear someone in the background saying, "Hey we're still on the phone, Davenport." Phoenix laughs and says, "Babe I'm on a conference call with investors in Russia and you got me talking dirty, I'll call you when I'm done." I could feel Phoenix's smile through the phone as he cooed, "Aww, you're thinking about me?" I return the smile and before I could answer him he says, "I know you are, that's why you called." "Good night mister, get back to your meeting." I heard a voice in the background say, "Yes, let's finish this meeting so we can get home to our loved ones." We say goodbye and hang up. What is it about this man that drives me crazy? Just the sound of his voice or being in his presence sends chills through my body and I have this uncontainable desire to be with him, to feel him, to smell and taste him. I really want to open up to Phoenix, but visions of my past keep popping in my head, preventing me from taking a leap of faith and allow myself to know how love really feels. I know now, I want love; I want someone to love me whole-heartedly, protect me, care for me, and to live happily ever after. Okay now I know I'm tripping because no one lives happily ever after. Drama and tragedy seem to follow me wherever I go and Phoenix has no idea who I am or what type of life I have lived. I wonder if he knew where I came from, what type of life I've lived would he still feel the same about me. Phoenix and I are so different, but they say, opposites attract. He has obviously lived a good life, with loving parents who raised him in a safe environment, cared and provided for him. Thank God, Amber was there to take care of me and Justin after my parents died. She did the best she could with what she was given but she was smart and focused. I'm glad she loved us enough to make sure we were safe and didn't abandon us. A big part of me feels she got the raw end of the deal by having to raise her younger siblings when she could have left us to the 'system'. What an enormous responsibility for her to take care of two kids, when she was still a kid herself. It was a blessing that the house was paid for and that my dad had money saved and stashed. She worked odd end jobs to make sure we ate and had clothes. School was very important to Amber and she made sure we went. When she graduated from high school she was given a full college scholarship. As I look back now, I'm really glad Amber did not lose sight of her hopes and dreams and was able to pursue a graduate degree and then a Ph.D. I'm very proud of her accomplishments but I wish she was able to have been a kid, a teen, and then a young adult. Instead she had to grow up much faster than she should have and missed out on a lot. She never partied, went on dates, or just hung out with friends. Her main focus in life was first us then her studies. She learned my father's hustle and business sense, therefore, she was able to take care of us and go to school. She did it...but the struggle was real! Justin and I are everlastingly grateful for what she did.

I wonder with Phoenix and I being so different if we can work, "Do I need to nip this in the bud before it gets too deep and I can't protect my heart?" I express out loud. After all that we went through, Amber was able to become successful in her career and found the man of her dreams. I often think about how she has found love and has completely given her heart to her husband. They appear to be very happy and she doesn't seem to let our past affect her life and her relationship. I watch the two of them interact and he clearly loves, cares, and respects her. I want the same, but will not be able to do so unless I can get past my troubled background. I did not go to college but I'm business savvy, all of which I learned at home and in the streets. Sometimes life is the best teacher and what I've learned and experienced, cannot be taught in a classroom or learned from a book.

Chapter fourteen

Justin, on the other hand, has another story. I know without a doubt he loves me and Amber unconditionally and will do anything for both of us. I wonder if he will really be able to love a woman for the simple fact that he never received the love a son should receive from his mother. Justin is very bitter towards women and has no respect for them, except for Amber and me. He feels that women owe him something when in fact the only woman that owed him anything was our mother. I pray one day he realizes that every woman is not like our mother and that there are some good women out there. He needs to realize this before it's too late and he spends the rest of his life alone. He also needs to re-evaluate the type of women he deals with because the last one was a real winner and I mean that in the most sarcastic way possible. Justin did not suffer the sexual abuse Amber and I did but he harbors just as many deep dark secrets and pain as we do. Killing a man at the tender age of 6-years-old is enough to drive anyone insane. Justin and Coco had a long-term relationship but he got jealous about her current profession and had issues with other men touching her in a sexual way. They ended their relationship with Justin giving her a black eye and she giving him a busted lip. I was glad Coco stood up for herself and handled her business by not allowing a man to physically abuse her even if it was my brother and when I saw him I slapped him so hard in the face somehow busting his other lip and let him know I will kick his ass if he puts his hands on another woman. I will not tolerate Justin hitting women. I remember the look he had on his face, he wanted to slap my ass back but he knew better. Thinking about Coco reminds me that I need to get to work and make some money…mama needs about five pair of new shoes!

When I make it to the club on Friday night, I pull in to a parking spot, kill the ignition and gather my thoughts to get mentally prepared to work tonight. I retrieve my cell phone and pull up Rocky's name. I send him a text message to let him know I was in the parking lot and needed help with my bags. He replies, "On my way." Within seconds he appears at my car gently knocking on the window. I unlock the car door and he opens it, leans in and kisses me on the cheek. It kind of took me by surprise, because the last time we were speaking he was yelling at me. I smile and say, "I'm glad to see you too babe." He extends his hand to help me exit the car. I hit the switch to pop the trunk so Rocky can retrieve my bags. I close the car door and head to the back of the car. Rocky grabs my bags, closes the trunk and I hit the alarm; the both of us head for the entrance of the club. The club is full as usual but the vibe is different. I see a lot of new faces and there's no one on stage, which is strange. "Why are the girls serving drinks and not working the stage?" I think to myself. I make my way to my dressing room after exchanging some smiles and saying hello. After unlocking my dressing room door, I walk in to find Delaney in my dressing room sitting in my chair. He smiles and stands to greet me. Delaney wraps his arms around me and squeezes me tight. I draw back a little and ask "Who died?" Delaney lets out a loud uncomfortable laugh and replies, "Nobody died Sydney, I'm just glad to see you, that's all." I tell Delaney to let me go and he's a horrible liar. There's a knock on the door. "Come in," I yell. Rocky enters my dressing room with a big smile plastered on his face. Delaney looks at me then at

Rocky and says, "Tomorrow we need to get together and talk about some business stuff." A look of concern appears on my face and Delaney picks up on my facial expression and tells me not to worry my pretty little head because it's all good. It's hot in this damn room. I take in a deep breath and express, "Delany you need to get some damn windows in the hell hole because the ventilation sucks and it smells like hot ass and sweaty balls!" Delaney and Rocky break out in laughter and Rocky asks, "Where does she get this shit from?" Delaney turns and heads for the door then turns around and says, "Sydney I had planned on calling you prior to you coming in to pre-warn you of tonight's events." I raise an eyebrow and say, "What's going on?" Delaney proceeds to tell me that the club is closed for a private bachelor party and not that he was surprised but I have been requested to be the main event so he was really glad that I showed up because he forgot to call me regarding the scheduled event. He continues to tell me that the bachelor and his boys are well aware of my fee, which is a minimum of five-thousand for my personal performance. Delaney hands me a sealed envelope and says, "I told them your fee tonight was five-thousand and they happily added another two-thousand without any argument. I didn't have a problem telling them that fee because they wipe their asses with money, they got so much. Don't worry about paying me anything because they also paid for me shutting down the club tonight, so I'm all good." "Who is the lucky husband-to-be?" I asked. I knew it had to be an actor or an athlete because they are generally the ones who pay this kind of money to close down a club. Delaney indicates the groom asked specifically for me. It's good to know that what I do has people personally asking for me. Delaney interjects, "He's a B-Ball player from Los Angeles. I'm leaving now so you can get ready because the girls on the floor can only hold them off for so long." I ask Delaney if Coco was here and he acknowledges with a head shake. "Please put her on the stage to get them pumped up and ready for me." "Done. Now get ready sugar and knock them dead." As Delaney exits he says, "make papa proud," he laughs and walks out. Rocky looks at me and says, "I got your back boo, do your thing and I'll see you out there." I give Rocky two thumbs up, blow him a kiss and he exits the room. I pull my clothes out of my bag to see what outfits I have for tonight's performance. A red hot lace teddy with a matching G-string and thigh-highs, the little number that ties right at the bust line showing just enough to make them want to see more; a black one-piece leather body/cat suit with the crotch and ass missing but very similar to the one Halle Berry wore in Catwoman, this outfit could expose my fresh Brazilian wax, and the firmness of my ass, if I don't wear my G-string; a white lace above the knee baby doll dress also with a matching G-string, lace push-up bra, and thigh-highs. I also have a naughty cheerleader outfit that might work for lap dances after my performance and how appropriate. I place the cheerleader outfit to the side so I don't have to search for it when I'm done. I selected the white outfit due to the occasion and begin to apply my makeup to match the outfit. As I am applying my makeup my cell phone rings, I glance at the caller I.D. and a huge smile appears on my face because it's Phoenix. I click the little green phone symbol on the phone and answer to the deepest sexiest voice on the other end. We speak for a few minutes and I tell him about the private party I'm getting ready for. Phoenix tells me to have a good time and become every man's fantasy, just don't give his honey away! He is laughing when he said it but somehow I know he meant it in a loving way and not in a jealous way. "Never... this is all yours babe," I reply. "Now that's what I wanted to hear," he sings on the other end. Before hanging up he asks if Ben can pick me up after the show. "Absolutely! I gotta go babe but I will see you later," I reply. I click off the phone so I can continue getting ready for my performance. It's almost showtime, the music is loud, and the chatter from the customers is louder. I'm preparing to put on a damn good show. I feel more comfortable with private shows at the club because there's more control and the men cannot get too much out of control. The athletes in particular can't control their hands especially if they've had alcohol. But you better know that Rocky will be there to check a fool in a New York minute. I slide into my red hot number which hugs my every curve much like it was imbedded and a part of my skin. I had to personally make sure it fit my body to a tee making sure my ass is firm and my ta-ta's stand at attention ready to slap some man in the face with their firmness. I love the catsuit, so I will make that my second outfit. I complete my transformation just as I hear my intro music start to play. I choose "Sex Me" by R. Kelly; of course 'R' is singing this song to women but my DJ is so amazing and talented with mixes that he transforms the song to fit my needs. I open the door to my dressing room, exit and make my way to the stage. As I slowly walk towards the stage I hear the music blaring louder in my ears and 'Honey', my alter ego, is about to take over! I hear the words of R. Kelly through his lyrics:

I feel so freaky tonight,

and I need someone to make me feel alright,

so bring your body here baby, baby have no fear,

I'm gonna fulfill your fantasies,

just as long as you....oh oh oh

Sex me baby, baby, come on, come on, come on!

As the words come through the speakers "I feel so freaky tonight" I stop walking and gyrate, moving my hips in a rotating motion; to the beat of the music, I caress my breasts, and take my hands and move them up and down my legs, squatting and bringing my hands to rub and rest on my 'centerpiece'... the room explodes in screams and hand claps. When R. Kelly says "I need someone to make me feel alright," I search for the man of the hour, the groom. I spot him across the room in a white T-shirt that has 'Groom' written across it. I make my way over to him keeping eye to eye contact along the way; I want to put him under my honey spell so I can have his undivided attention. As I approach the groom, he is sitting in the middle of the floor in a high-back chair. I extend my arm in the air to give the DJ a signal to replay the last verse of the song. I'm standing in front of the groom and gently take his hands and place them on my breasts, he didn't waste any time grabbing them and hungrily squeezing them. I straddle him and start grinding his manhood! He's ready, I thought, even before I straddled him. He removes his hands from my breasts and replaces them with my ass cheeks, holding on for dear life. I grind on him and he's looking in my eyes, I take my right index finger and run it across my centerpiece, flickering my finger to capture my natural scent, surely to drive the groom wild. I remove my finger and place it under his nose to give him a whiff of my sweet nectar, then outlining his lips with my finger damn near sends his ass overboard because he didn't know what hit him. Not only am I driving this man crazy, the crowd is going wild with screams and whistles. Again, just the fuel I need to make this the performance of a lifetime. I'm dancing for this man and I'm thinking about Phoenix and what I want to do to him tonight. One guys yells, "Bring your fine ass over here! I won't stare at you like that fool, I will be handling my business with yo ass!" My mind is on the groom, I look down at him as he is in pure shock, he won't take his eyes off of me, it's like I hypnotized him with my moves. I lean in closer to the groom and whisper in his ear "breathe baby" I back up to continue my performance with some of the other guests. I'll move back to the groom after he has regained his composure. I make my way around the club before hitting the dance floor. I climb up on the stage and give the DJ my cue to change my music so I can get nasty for the boys. I look over at the groom who still has his eyes on me and give him the finger in a "come here" motion. He stands and starts to walk in my direction, it's like he's floating in the air like in one of those Spike Lee movies when the people look like they're floating instead of walking. I signal Rocky to bring a chair on the stage so the groom can sit on the stage front and center. Rocky complies and places the chair on stage. The light hits the groom's face and I get a good look at his chiseled features for the first time. This man is fine as hell. He is like a tall, thick glass of chocolate milk. His dark milk chocolate skin is smooth and creamy. He had round-almond, deep dark brown eyes that are quite captivating. His smile is wide with beautiful white teeth. His hands are soft not like a ball player but more like a man who has a desk job. He has black hair with loose ringlets; his feature resembles someone who is of East Indian, African-American and maybe Italian heritage. I'm not sure but he has very exotic features. I look out in the crowd and notice some of the Bay Area's finest are in the house. I see some rappers, entertainers, actors and ball players. I notice a rapper and really good friend, who has some classic club songs; he blows a kiss to me and winks his eye. Just on cue, the DJ switches my music to a real upbeat booty shaking song. I move to the edge of the stage and drop it like it's hot so the crowd can see Honey up close and personal. I hear one guy scream "I love you Honey! Will you be my baby mama?" I laugh and continue my performance. "Shake That Monkey" by Too Short comes screaming through the speakers and it is like fuel for the crowd. Again, I hear screams, whistles, and clapping. I walk back to the center of the stage, where my groom is sitting waiting patiently for my return. I stand in front of him and remove my cat suit leaving my black lace G-string and my seven-inch "come fuck me" pumps on. Since the crowd is clapping for me it's time for me to make it clap for them. I turn my back to the crowd and with the beat of the music I make my ass cheeks dance to their own beat. I look back at the groom who is now leaning over the chair trying to get a glimpse of me shaking my monkey... so to speak. A multitude of men come up to the stage and make it rain like there's no tomorrow. I never miss a beat and the DJ does a quick switch and blast, "Drop And Give Me Fifty" by Mike Jones, I think to myself this boy is working for his money tonight and playing all my jams. I gave him a CD at the beginning of my show but sometimes he goes off on his own and plays what he thinks I should dance to, I just roll with it because he has never steers me in the wrong direction. The DJ gets on the mic and asks the crowd "what ya'll want her to do?" and simultaneously they all yell "drop and give me fifty!" I comply with the crowd's request and drop to the floor with my legs spread eagle and make my ass bounce like one of the ball players dribbles a basketball down the court. The groom jumps out of his chair, throws his hands in the air and starts to sing along with the words of the song as did the crowd. I stand up and perform to the words of the song;

"put your right hand in the air, put the left one in your underwear

now tickle that kat, tickle that kat".

There has to be at least a hundred guys in the club tonight and they are on 'full' and out of control. I motion for the groom to sit back in the chair on the stage, he follows my instructions. I position the chair so he is facing the crowd; it's time for me to slow this performance down and right on cue the DJ plays 'Say Yes' by the Whispers. As the smooth sounds float through the speakers, I make eye contact with the groom again and seductively dance in front of him, cupping my breasts in my hands, squeezing my nipples, he is hypnotized yet again. I move closer and straddle him, gently and slowly grinding my centerpiece against his legs. The groom grabs my ass and pulls me closer forcefully. I turn my head and look back at Rocky who knows my signal and within seconds, Rocky is on stage with a black silk scarf and ties the groom's hands behind the chair. Once his hands are nice and secure behind his back, I continue my performance. I place my hands on his outer thighs and pull them close together, exposing a few inches on both sides of the chair. I stop dancing, back away from the groom a little, placing my legs in front of his. I then bend over with my ass pointing to the crowd, place my hands on the chair getting a tight grip on both sides, with the quickness I am doing a handstand on the chair with the groom under me. The crowd explodes! My legs are straight in the air and my ass is directly in the groom's face; I'm sure he can smell what I had for breakfast. I lower my head and place my mouth directly on his manhood, which is still budging in his pants and shake my head to give him some added pleasure, this man is hard as a rock. He starts to wiggle like he had to pee, I tell him, "Be still or you are going to make me fall." He stops moving and I slowly start to spread my legs, doing the splits in midair. He lowers his head trying to rest his face on my centerpiece. I close my legs at the right time because this fool was about to try and lick me between my legs. He says, "Damn baby you smell like honey and I want to lick your honey jar." I ignore his request and bring my legs down to stand. I turn to the crowd and bow. I receive a standing ovation. I turn to the groom and sit on his lap reaching my hands around to the back of the chair to untie his hands. My exit song,

Trina's, 'Shake Wit It', is now coming through the speakers. I hug the groom, kiss him on the cheek and whisper in his ear; "congratulations on getting married." He hugs me back and says, "Girl you know you got me fucked up right now? Thank you for that wonderful performance; you were all that and a bag of chips! I heard you were good, but you blew me away. Thanks again for making my last night as a single man well worth it. I gave the owner your fee but you deserve much more. If I wasn't getting married...I would tap that ass!" I laugh, "I know boo that's what they all say." He stands, reaches in his pocket and pulls out a wad of cash. He hands the cash to me, kisses me on the cheek and walks away shaking his head. I turn to the crowd once again before I make my exit and I get another standing ovation. Guys are still standing at the edge of the stage still making it rain. I sing to myself in my Ice Cube voice, "today was a good day". I exit the stage and head to my dressing room and I feel hands grabbing me. I look back for Rocky and see him on the stage with Coco retrieving my stuff and the cash I left behind. He sees me looking back and says something to Coco and jumps off the stage. The men are out of control and their hands are octopuses' with arms coming at me from all directions. Rocky now trails me telling the men to back the hell off. I finally make it to my dressing room. I quickly pick up my phone off the vanity to send Phoenix a text to let him know I am done for the night and he can send Ben to get me now. Before I could hit the send button, my phone dinged letting me know I had a text message.

Chapter fifteen

Phoenix was sending me a text as I was sending him one. He informs me that Ben is waiting outside for me when I'm ready and he can't wait to see me. Coco and Rocky are coming through the door. Coco starts running around the room like she has lost her mind screaming, "Sydney, damn girl you did the damn thing tonight! Girl you were in rare form....what's gotten into you?" I laugh and respond, "I was just doing my job babe, making men happy and making money!" Speaking of money, Rocky is sitting in the chair counting my earnings for the night. I pull my hair back in a tight ponytail, put some Victoria's Secret sweatpants and a hoodie on, so I'm comfortable. Coco stops running around enough to help me put my stuff in my duffle. She has so much energy tonight, she reminds me of the little pink energizer bunny, but she talks instead of banging on a drum. I give Rocky the wad of cash the groom gave me to add to the pile. He looks at me and says, "Where did this come from?" "The groom," I reply. Rocky takes the money and adds it to the rest. I grab the envelop Delaney gave me earlier and wait for Rocky to tell me how much I made. Coco starts up again, she's yelling, "Girl I don't think we've ever had that much money in the club in one night! I mean, we get the occasional athlete, rapper, and actor, but damn that Los Angeles groom brought all the big ballers out tonight. I guess that's why he closed the club tonight so it would be exclusive, I'm not mad at him. I heard the regulars were pissed they couldn't come in tonight. Delaney let Ben in though. Thank you so much Sydney for letting me open for you. Lord knows I couldn't afford to be off tonight. I made about six-hundred." Oh shit, Ben saw my performance, I thought. "Don't mention it girl, you know I got your back." Rocky sat very quiet, still counting my earnings, he then mumbles something. I turn and ask, "What did you say?" He repeats something but I still didn't understand him. "What did you say Rocky?" When he repeats himself, I detected a bit of an attitude. "You made forty-eight hundred in tips and another three-thousand from the groom." He stands and hands me the stack of cash. Coco screams, "Did you say she made seventy-eight hundred?" "Yeah that's what I said," again with an attitude. "Rocky I heard you the first time. I was being funny, where's your sense of humor tonight?" He speaks in a dry voice, "I lost it, and maybe you can help me get it back." Coco puts her hands on her hips and shouts, "Well if you keep that attitude maybe I won't mister!" I take a glance around the room to make sure I'm not leaving anything. I made almost fifteen thousand dollars tonight…indeed tonight was a good night and not bad for a couple of hours of work! Before we all walk, I ask Coco and Rocky to wait a second. I count fifteen hundred dollars, hand it to Coco and thank her again for all the help tonight. She covers her mouth and tears well in her eyes. "Thank you so much Syd, you have no idea how much I need this." "Yes I do, that's why you have it mama. I told you if you need anything to let me know, because if I have it, you have it." Then I count out two-thousand and hand it to Rocky. He looks at me funny and asks, "Why are you giving me money? Delaney already took care of me?" "Because you are my boy and I appreciate all you do for me. Now stick the damn money in your pocket and let's go." I pick up my duffle, drape it over my shoulder and we all walk out. Rocky takes my bag, smiles at me then heads for the exit." Rocky made it to the exit and when he opened the front door, his facial expression changed again. I got to the front door and saw Ben standing out there with the back passenger door open, apparently waiting for me. He pops the trunk and Rocky walks over and places my bag inside and closes the trunk. He has really been acting strange lately; I will have to catch up with him tomorrow to find out what's bothering him. Rocky thanks me again for the 'bonus', kisses me on the cheek, tells me he loves me and heads back towards the entrance to the club. I yell to him, "That's for watching the boys for me and for always watching my back." He laughs and says, "I will always have your back Syd, and I have no problem watching the boys for you, however, I might have to start charging you because that Teddy is one bad ass dog." "I know he is and you love him anyway!" I reply. "This is true but it doesn't remove the fact that his ass is bad," he laughs as he walks back in the club. Ben holds out his hand to help me in the back seat. He closes the door and walks around to the driver side, gets in and closes his door. Ben starts the engine and pulls forward to exit the club's parking lot. Just as we pull out of the parking lot, a car flies past us and slams on his brakes, which causes Ben to slam on his brakes to prevent from plowing into the back of him. Ben yells, "What the hell is wrong with this idiot?" The car stops and doesn't move for several seconds. Ben lays on the car's horn but the other car doesn't move. Ben then puts the car in park and tells me he'll be right back, he wants to see what the hell is this fool's problem. Just as Ben steps out the car, the car speeds away leaving a trail of smoke behind. Ben gets back in the car apparently upset at the juvenile antics of the person in the other car. Ben straightens his black suit jacket and looks in the mirror and asks, "Are you okay Ms. Sydney?" I reply, "Yes I am. Do you have any idea who that is?" "I have no idea Ms. Sydney but whoever it is they have royally pissed me off." Ben apologizes to me. "Please don't apologize. I completely understand you're upset, and it's not your fault this maniac is playing games with us." For the next hour and a half, Ben and I ride in silence. It normally only takes thirty minutes to drive from Oakland to the city but there was some major traffic on the Bay Bridge due to an accident. Ben's car phone rings and he reaches up to the mirror to click the talk button. He answers, "Mr. Davenport?" Phoenix's voice comes over the speaker asking Ben is everything alright? Ben replies, "There's a bit of traffic on the Bay Bridge but we should be pulling up shortly." Phoenix then says, "Hello babe." "Hey yourself," I reply. Ben interjects and informs Phoenix we are exiting the bridge. I say to him, "I will see you soon." He replies, "I'll be waiting." and the phone goes dead. We finally pull up to the Fairmount Hotel. Ben is still visibly upset. He exits the car, retrieves my bag from the trunk, and then helps me out. As I exit the car, Ben and I hear an engine roaring in back of us. We both look in the direction of the car making the unnecessary noise and Ben says. "Oh shit, did this asshole just follow us?" Ben asks. "Ms. Sydney, please get back in the car for a second so I can get to the bottom of this nonsense." Ben proceeds to walk towards the car and once again the car speeds off burning rubber and leaving a cloud of smoke. Ben comes back to the car and opens the door to let me out. "Did you get a chance to see the driver?" I asked. "No, the window was too dark making it impossible to see who is behind the wheel." Ben tells me he will let Mr. Davenport know I am on my way up. I reach the automatic glass doors when I hear Ben call my name. I turn to him and he blurts out, "Quite an amazing performance tonight. You are truly talented!" I smile, say thank you, and proceed through the doors to have some much anticipated time with Phoenix. I really can't wait to see him. I'm on the elevator when my cell phone dings indicating I have a text message. I retrieve my phone from my hoody pocket to see who's texting me at this hour. The message is from Phoenix letting me know that the front door is open and to just come on in. As I approach the front door I can hear jazz playing. I grab the door handle and enter the apartment. I am hit with the amazing aroma of vanilla and an array of candles placed throughout the house. There is a pathway of candles leading to the bedroom. I follow the candles and when I reach the bedroom Phoenix is not there. I then see a light under the closed door of the bathroom so I drop my duffle bag in the sitting area and proceed in the direction of the bathroom. I call out to him and he responds that he's in the bathroom and he wants me to join him. I enter the bathroom and I am greeted with more jazz, candles surrounding the bathtub, and Phoenix sitting in the bathtub with red rose pedals floating on top of the bubbles. A glass of wine in his hand, and an additional glass on the side of the tub I presume for me. Phoenix smiles at me and says, "Hello sexy, please join me". I stand there for a second looking at the gorgeous man in the tub. I have no idea what he has over me but I like it so I sit on the toilet to remove my shoes. He requests that I remove my clothes slowly so he can watch me and observe how beautiful I am; I comply with his request. I remove the last piece of clothing and move towards the bathtub. I step up the two steps then down two steps to join this beautiful man in the bathtub. The water is hot, not too hot that it will burn my skin but comfortably hot. I sit down, positioning myself between his legs. I rest my head on his chest and let out a deep sigh. He clicks a button on a small remote and the wall opens, exposing a small fireplace in front of us. He clicks another button and a fire appears instantly. I sink deeper into his chest not ever wanting leave. There are slow moving jets hitting different places on my body. This is so relaxing. He kisses me on the side of my neck, hands me a glass of wine and says, "Welcome home babe." Phoenix and I sit relaxing in the bathtub for the next 45 minutes before he says, "Babe let's get out and get ready for bed." I didn't realize how tired I was because I drifted into a light slumber resting against Phoenix's chest...the rhythm of his heart beat relaxed me so that I fell asleep. I step out of the bathtub and Phoenix follows. He hands me a bath skirt off the shelf next to the sink then grabs one for himself. We both dry off our bodies in silence. I reach down to gather my clothes off the floor and he tells me to leave them, grabs my hand and leads me out of the bathroom. Once in the bedroom, he removes the decorative pillows and places them neatly on the floor, pulls back the goose down comforter and gently lays me down and covers my naked body. He moves to the other side of the bed and joins me under the covers. He moves close and hugs me, kisses me on the forehead then tells me to rest. I ask Phoenix if he's okay because he's been pretty quiet and reserved this evening. He tells me he wants me to rest and that he's concerned for my safety.

I look at him and ask, "Where is this coming from?" He hesitates for a moment then informs me that he had a conversation with Ben and he reiterated the events of the evening with the mysterious car. Phoenix expresses he does not want me to dance anymore because he's afraid I have a crazed stalker. I laugh, "Babe I appreciate your concern but I've been dancing for a while and have come across many special people but never a crazed stalker." "There's a first time for everything Sydney and this is not a laughing matter." he replies. My attitude slightly changes because this conversation sort of reminds me of one with Cameron. I will not be controlled and told what to do. However, Cameron didn't want me to continue dancing because he was jealous, whereas, Phoenix cares for me and is concerned for my safety which makes it different. I shake the thought of control out of my head and replace it with that of love and concern. He then says something that catches me completely off guard. He expresses that he has fallen in love with me, wants me to be his wife, and the mother of his children. Therefore, he needs to take every measure to make sure I am safe and protected from any danger. Okay, pump your breaks tuffy, I am not about to be anyone's mother I think to myself.

I look deep into Phoenix's eyes and tell him I am enjoying him and the time that we've spent and are spending together but I am not made out to be anyone's mother. I don't have it in me nor do I want the responsibility of being anyone's mother. Phoenix grabs my chin and passionately kisses me; he looks in my eyes and enlightens me by saying, "you need to allow yourself to love and trust babe. I've fallen in love with you and I know you feel something for me.

If not love, a deep like", he chuckles. "You will be the perfect wife and mother, you need to open up and believe that not everyone is out to get you or to hurt you." "I'm flattered Phoenix, but you don't know me. You have no idea who I am and what deep dark shit that's in my past that will prevent me from being a part of your dream. I think we should end this now before we get too deep and I end up being a disappointment to you." Phoenix is still staring at me and has this slight grin on his face. I'm glad he thinks this shit is amusing. I convey that we are from two different worlds and that he's way too good for me and maybe he needs to find someone who will share his dreams of being a wife and mother. As I say this, I think that deep down inside, this is what I truly want but the chances of it happening are probably slim to none. This is some scary shit and I don't believe I can handle it. I can feel a panic attack coming on. I remove the covers and try to exit the bed but Phoenix grabs my arm, not in an aggressive way but with enough force to pull me back down. "Phoenix please don't, just let me go," I request. He does not let go of my arm and once again I am sitting on the bed. He moves closer to me and says, "Sydney why won't you let me in? From the moment I saw you at the club, I was drawn in by your beauty babe, not just the outer but the inner beauty that resides inside you. We all go through things in our lives but we learn from them and pray that God moves us and makes us better people. I always remember what my mother said...what doesn't kill you, will make you stronger. I know you don't believe this, but when I first laid eyes on you it was love at first sight. I knew you were the woman I've been praying for. Everything happens for a reason, people are put in your life for a reason." I'm staring at him, listening and fighting tears from falling down my cheeks. He continues, "Yes, it's devastating that I lost my parents and my sister but *God* kept me in perfect peace. *He* brought Ben in my life, who is just not my driver but my best friend and I trust him with my life. I can't begin to express the love I have for my aunt. She told me that the moment she saw you and had that first conversation with you in the kitchen that she knew you were the one for me. Babe, it's that inner beauty I'm speaking about. Maybe you don't know you have it but it radiates around you all the time. That's what my aunt saw in you, just as I did and she didn't see you swinging around a pole." He chuckles. I have lost this battle, the tears are now flowing and I can't stop them. Why does this man make me feel like this? I don't want to admit it, but I think I have fallen in love with Phoenix Davenport! He then reminds me that I told him I didn't need a 'Captain Save a Hoe'. "Babe I'm not here to save you, I'm here to love you unconditionally and protect you. I really want you to drop this protective shield you have around your heart and let me in. I will not leave you nor will I hurt you, I just want to love you if you give me a chance." I'm crying uncontrollably now and I really don't want him to see me like this. I have all these feelings that are emerging and I can't control them. I try to move once again but he holds me. "Sydney, what do I need to do to prove I will not hurt you?" "Let me go, please." Phoenix releases my arm and allows me to get up from the bed. I start to gather my things to get dressed when he stands and backs me up against the wall. He tells me with tears in his eyes that he doesn't want me to leave; he never wants me to leave. At this point tears are flowing like a river. I have to get out of here I think to myself. Phoenix restrains me which prevents me from moving, again not in an aggressive manner but more loving. I beg Phoenix to move and let me leave. He says, "Baby I can't. I need you just as much as you need me." "I don't need any fucking body! I can take care of myself, now get the fuck out of my way!" I scream. "You can get as mad as you want but you are not leaving." I start to beat on his chest to make him move but he remains still and doesn't move. I beat on his chest until I am out of energy and fall to the floor. Phoenix falls to the floor with me and holds me tight until I stop crying which seems like hours. He wipes away my tears and reports that I needed to get that out of my system. He expresses that he wants to know what's going on because he's not going anywhere and he will be ready to listen when I'm ready to talk. "I am here to help you fight whatever you are going through, help you release whatever demons that are holding you back from having true love," he says with so much passion. Exhausted and hoarse from crying, I muster up enough energy to say, "There is no hope for me Phoenix." He declares that there is hope I just need to believe there is. "You're beautiful, intelligent, and an amazing woman. I believe you've had a certain way of thinking which prevents you to feel, love, and trust or care for anyone really outside of your close friends and family. Once you change your way of thinking, things will make sense and you will start to feel different about life," he expresses. He informs me that he believes in me and that I should start believing in myself as well. "I feel like I'm a bad luck charm and every time I get involved or try to open up with someone it never ends well," I express. "Sydney I want all of you, the good the bad and the ugly. I'm not concerned about your past; I'm only concerned with our future," he says. I take a deep breath and say, "Okay let's get back in bed because it doesn't look like you're letting me go anytime soon and I feel like a crazy person crying on the floor." I think to myself, maybe it's time for me to step out on faith and tell him everything about me and if he leaves me it's understandable…I will move on.

Chapter sixteen

We move to the bed and back under the covers, there's a dead silence. I start my story by indicating, "unlike you Phoenix, I grew up in a very dysfunctional family. My parents were street hustlers that had 3 children they probably shouldn't have had. Anyway, there was an endless amount of traffic, drugs, and alcohol in our house. My parents were more concerned with what they could get out of people than protecting their own children. Unfortunately due to their lack of parenting and protection, my sister and I were molested and raped at a very young age and my brother ended up killing a man trying to protect us. This ultimately resulted in retaliation and the murder of my parents. Now, you have my screwed up life all summed up in a nut shell." Phoenix remains quiet with his head down staring at his hands. He then moves closer to me, still not saying a word but wraps his arms around me and holds on to me for dear life. He strokes my hair and kisses my cheek, chin, and forehead. We slid down in the bed, burying ourselves with the covers; I am dead tired and just want to close my eyes and go to sleep. This has proven to be a very mentally and emotionally draining day for me. As we lay in each other arms, Phoenix whispers in my ear, "Sydney, I love you and I will protect you, please allow me to do that." He rubs my stomach and whispers, "I will also love and protect our babies!" I am too tired to respond to his last comment. My eyelids are so heavy, I think I'm dreaming…I must be dreaming because he did not just say he will love and protect our babies! What the fuck! I scream in my head. My head weighs a ton and my mouth won't open, I know I'm dreaming, yes I must be dreaming because this is some nonsense he just said. I roll over and reach for Phoenix and feel an empty spot. I open my eyes to find the room still dark. I glance over at the nightstand to see the bright red digital numbers on the clock and it reads 1:30. Why is he up at 1:30am? He's probably working, I think to myself. I get out the bed and go to the bathroom to pee. Once done, I laid back in the bed and guess I drift off again because I can hear dogs barking. I hop up. Oh dear Lord, how could I have forgotten about my boys? I throw on Phoenix's robe to go and find him to let him know I need to go home because I didn't go home after the show and the dogs didn't eat. I walk down the hallway and it's bright. Shit, it's not 1:30am, it's 1:30pm. I hear the TV on so I follow the voices. I reach the living room and there sat Ben, Phoenix, Snickers and Teddy. Auntie Hattie is moving about in the kitchen. I stood there for a second. When Teddy sees me, he jumps off the couch and runs to me barking. Everyone looks up and Phoenix says, "Good afternoon sweetheart." "Hey everyone," I responded. "Babe why did you let me sleep this long?" I ask. "You were tired and obviously needed to rest. Did we wake you?" he replies. "No I was dreaming that I forgot about the dogs and that's what woke me up but I see that has been taken care of." Ben yells, "These two are my new little buddies, I love them." He explains how he notices that Snickers is very laid back and doesn't have a care in the world, whereas, Teddy is high-strung and has way too much energy. Aunt Hattie sings from the kitchen that she's fed them boiled chicken and steamed rice. Oh dear, am I still sleep because this is like a dream! I look at Phoenix sitting on the couch with some basketball shorts on reading the newspaper, and sipping some tea…he looks sexy as hell. He looks up at me and asks, "Did you sleep well?" I smile a very uncomfortable smile seeing as though I did just spill out my guts to this man last night, and nod yes. What does he have that makes me so comfortable, so safe and secure I ask myself? I don't know but I want to give myself a chance of finding out. I turn to get dressed and he calls for me. "Where are you going?" "To get dressed," I reply. He pats the seat next to him for me to come and sit. I comply. "I need to put some clothes on, you have guests," I whisper. "Guests? You are amongst family dear, you're fine. Relax, today is all about relaxing." "I'd feel a little more comfortable if I had on some clothes instead of your robe," I express. He nods and says "Whatever makes you happy babe." He leans in and plants a soft kiss on my lips and I instantly heat up. It's interesting how we can lay next to each other, sleep in each other's arms and not have sex. Aunt Hattie yells from the kitchen, "Lunch will be ready shortly." I make my way down the hall back to the master suite when Aunt Hattie calls my name. I turn around and make it halfway back when she meets me halfway. "Sweetheart, I wanted you to know that I'm happy you are in our lives. My nephew has apparently fallen in love with you. I see the way he looks at you and talks about you. He is my life and I ask that you don't break his heart. He's had enough heartbreaks and could not withstand anymore...understand?" She stares at me with compassion as well as seriousness. "Yes mama, I have no intentions of breaking his heart," was all I could say. "Good" she sings, kisses me on the cheek and pivots on her toes and returns to the kitchen. I stand there for a few more seconds then proceed to the master suite. I enter the bathroom and turn on the shower. I remove the robe and think "what heartbreak was she speaking of? Did another woman break his heart?" I wondered. I push it out of my mind and step into the shower and let the hot water wash my worries away. After showering and slipping into a comfortable Juicy sweatsuit, I return to the living room. I sit next to Phoenix and reach for his left hand to hold. He turns, looks at me then smiles. Aunt Hattie calls for us to come and eat. It's funny because Snickers was sleeping in Ben's lap but when he heard "eat"; he jumped up and ran in the kitchen…how easy they have adapted to their surroundings. Phoenix and I stand and make our way to the kitchen. Aunt Hattie has outdone herself again. She prepared smothered chicken, rice and gravy, yams, black-eyed peas and a green salad. There was also a German chocolate cake and peach cobbler for dessert. Ben says grace,

"Dear Lord, I want to take this time to thank you for this food we are about to receive and may it be nourishing to our bodies. Father, I ask that you bless this family and protect all of us from any harm or danger. I thank you for allowing Phoenix to find true love and I hope Aunt Hattie and I find it too! I thank you and praise you,

AMEN!

Aunt Hattie playfully smacks Ben on the arm; we all laugh and dig in. The food must be really good because everyone at the table is quiet. All you hear is the clicking of forks to plates. I finally say, "My goodness, this is the best food I have ever had." Aunt Hattie smiles and says, "Get used to it sweetheart because I need to keep you fed." Okay, I thought to myself, not sure what she meant by that but if it keeps her making this damn good food then so be it. Ben is helping Aunt Hattie with the dishes and Phoenix and I go back to the living room and sit on the couch. "Babe, how did you get the boys?" I asked. "I called Rocky to rescue the dogs for you. You were sleeping so soundly, I didn't want to wake you babe. I hope you don't mind that I called Rocky. Ben met with him and brought them here. You're a package deal," he smiles and kisses me." Still with a hoarse voice, I replied, "Thank you very much, that means a lot." I feel uncomfortable about our conversation last night and want to say something. It's amazing how he picks up on certain things about me, it's like he's reading my mind or maybe reading my facial expressions. He interrupts my thoughts and says, "We never have to talk about your past again unless we're in therapy and it's for healing purposes." I remain quiet once again trying to process all that is going on in my head and in my heart. My stomach decides to growl loud enough for Phoenix to hear. He turns to me and says, "Was that your stomach? You can't be hungry, you just ate." "It must be my nerves, because I'm not hungry." I lied because even though I just ate, I could have eaten again.

We're all relaxing in the living room. Ben is playing with the boys, Aunt Hattie is chatting with someone on her cell phone, Phoenix is watching TV and I'm reading a book on my iPad called 'Child of a Crack Head' by Shameek Speight. All of a sudden I feel sick to my stomach and feel like I need to throw up. I reach over to the coffee table and grab a peppermint and pop it in my mouth. Sometimes the mints settle my stomach. Everyone is doing their own thing when Ben announces he's going to cut out so he can take care of a few things. Aunt Hattie has finished her conversation and indicates she was going to take off as well. Phoenix lets them out, comes back to the couch and says, "Alone at last." He kisses me passionately, rubbing my thighs at the same time. He speaks, "I hear you put on quite a show last night." I give him a shy smile and ask, "Where on earth did you hear that?" He smiles, "Ben of course. It must have been out of this world because when he was describing the show, his eyes were big as apples and he was talking like he had seen a bright shiny new bike in the window and he was so excited that he was stuttering when talking. I was amused and got a kick out of his description of your show. Which brings me to another point, I am very uncomfortable that someone is following you and I want you to have a bodyguard." "A bodyguard? I am not Whitney Houston. I think you are blowing this way out of proportion and overreacting a little." "I don't think so Sydney. With the last episode being last night and the other incidents, I'm concerned." "What other incidents?" I ask. "Rocky mentioned that there have been a few other occurrences and he and I agree that you need protection when you're not with either one of us. Do you think this is a coincidence Sydney? I don't think so." He said in a concerned tone. Before I could answer, he told me I will have a bodyguard; it's the best thing to do. "Rocky and I will feel comfortable knowing that you have protection if you are not with one of us." "Phoenix, I am not a rock star and I do not need protection." He looks deep into my eyes, stands up and cups my face with his hands, kisses me deeply and says, "Woman, I love you and I love the fact that you're strong, but you will have a bodyguard and that's the end of that." The forcefulness of his voice turns me on. I pull away from him because my stomach is turning again. "What's wrong babe?" he questions. "I don't feel so well, I need to lie down." I start to walk in the direction of the master suite when I felt the need to run to make it to the bathroom before I throw up everywhere. I make it the bathroom just in time to release whatever has my stomach upset. Phoenix comes in shortly behind me with a concerned look on his face. He wets a washcloth and hands it to me. I wash my face and sit next to the toilet, trying to figure out why my stomach is upset. He looks over at me and says, "My babies got you sick already." "Okay, enough of the baby talk!" I shout. "You mentioned something about babies last night and now you're saying it again. Why is it that you keep bringing this up? I get that you have fallen in love with me and I am certainly feeling a way about you…but a baby let alone BABIES, it's not going to happen. My doctors have told me that due to the trauma my body sustained at a young age, that having children might be slim to none," I say, obviously annoyed. I am overwhelmed by emotions and tears begin to fall once again. This is like a replay; Phoenix wraps his arms around me as I cry like a baby. I pull away from him quickly because I need to throw up again. Once I wipe my mouth, I rest my back against the wall. I look at him and say, "I can get used to the idea of falling in love with you and having you fall in love with me, but if you want children, we can end this right now because I will not be able to give them to you and even if I could I wouldn't want to because being a mother is not in the cards for me." Phoenix looks at me with those dreamy eyes, kisses me on the forehead and says, "I've already fallen in love with you and it's too late mama, because you will have my kids…..a girl who will look just like me and a boy who will look just like you." Okay, now I know he has lost his mind and didn't hear a word I just said. "Why do you think you are sitting on the floor of my bathroom gripping the 'porcelain god'?" "Because something I ate didn't agree with me," I say with conviction. "Okay, you can go with that if you like, but I think otherwise." He stands and leaves the bathroom. I'm sitting on the floor looking like a deer caught in headlights. The thought of being pregnant makes me totally sick to my stomach and I throw up once again. I finally get off the floor, wash my face, brush my teeth and make my way to the bed to lie down. Phoenix is lying on the bed with his shirt off watching T.V. I climb in bed and snuggle up next to him. We watch T.V. in silence with him periodically looking at me and kissing me, we don't say a word to each other. At some point I roll over and fall asleep. I stretch some hours later; did I sleep all night again? Why am I so darn tired lately? I ask myself. Phoenix is not in bed so I get up to find him. I open the bedroom door and I am hit with a heavenly smell and my stomach instantly growls. I walk down the hall and I hear the news on the TV and Phoenix singing in the kitchen. "Good morning handsome," I sing as I approach the bar table. He turns to me and asks if I am hungry." I walk over to him, give him a hug, and my stomach growls again but loud enough for him to hear. I giggle, "I guess so because it sounds like I haven't eaten in a month." He picks up two plates off the counter and starts to fill them with food. I walk around and sit at the bar and wait patiently for my food. I look through the living room to the balcony and see the

153

boys lying out there on beds with black sweaters on. I turn to look at Phoenix and he says, "Aunt Hattie brought a bag of stuff for them this morning. For the life of me I can't understand why people dress dogs in clothes," he laughs. He places a plate in front of me and one to the left of me for him. He has prepared a cheese, bacon, spinach, and mushroom omelet, sour dough toast and a glass of orange juice. I wait for him to sit beside me so we can eat together. Phoenix takes his seat next to me and grabs my hand to bless the food. After we eat, I start to clean the kitchen. He tells me to leave it, because the cleaning lady will be there today. He informs me that he has to go into the office today but he wants me to go shopping. He hands me his Black American Express Card and says, "Spare no expense." You don't have to tell me twice. I kiss him and we head to the bathroom to shower together. I dress, grab my purse and head for the door.

Chapter seventeen

I exit the hotel double doors to find Ben waiting for me with the back passenger door open. "Good afternoon Ms. Sydney," he greets me. I smile, give him a peck on the cheek and reply to his greeting. Ben closes my door and enters the driver's side, closes his door, starts the engine, then lets down the window's sub-divider to see me. When the divider came down I realized there was someone else in the car. Ben looks at me in the rear-view mirror and introduces me to my new bodyguard 'X'. I speak, "Hello X, I'm Sydney. I appreciate you being here but it's really not necessary. Ben and I are just going to do a little shopping." I'm not sure how tall X is but he seems to be a pretty large man. I would guess that he's stands about 6'5 and about 290 pounds. X turns in the seat to face me, and says, "I like shopping; we're going to have fun" and then claps his hands. Wow, he's a smart ass, just what I need. He has a deep voice that reminds me of James Earl Jones in the 'Lion King'. He appears to be of Pacific Island decent because he looks Samoan or Hawaiian. His olive skin tone is flawless, his round-almond eyes are black like onyx and his lips are nice and full. He has jet black hair that's pulled back in a tight ponytail centered at the back of his head and twisted in a bun. I tell X that it is really not necessary that he go with Ben and I. Without turning around in his seat, X simply said, "With all due respect Ms. Sydney, I am here to protect you from any harm and I work for Mr. Davenport. I will take my instructions from him and him alone. So please, sit back, relax and tell Ben where we are shopping today." Well I guess he told me. "Ben, I guess we're all shopping at Union Square today." X then leans forward and hits the switch that raises the window's sub-divider. Who the hell does this oversize asshole think he's talking to? I say to myself. I am beyond irritated. Phoenix has got to be kidding me with this shit, and he has a lot of nerve just springing this on me and not allowing my input in who he hires. If he wanted to hire someone to protect me full time then he could have given the job to Rocky, someone I completely trust! I pull my cell phone out of my purse and dial his number. He answers on the first ring. "You are full of surprises aren't you?" I shout. He laughs and says, "Babe have fun shopping, please buy whatever you like and don't give X a hard time, he's a nice guy." Still irritated, "Whatever, you'll pay for this when you get the bill! And he's not nice; he's a giant sarcastic asshole!" I shout. Again, Phoenix laughs and says, "I can handle whatever damage you do." He then tells me he needs me to do him a favor. "Yes, what is it?" I ask. "Today is Ben's birthday, so show him some love and pick up something nice from the both of us." "Okay I will but I'm still mad at you." I comment. "I love you too. He likes 'time pieces' so again, use your creativity and spare no expense," he says. I tell him okay. He says he loves me again and hangs up the phone. I text my sister, Rocky, and Coco to see what they are up to; Coco was the only one who responded quickly. We exchanged a few messages and I told her I was on my way to Union Square to do a little damage and she tells me she wishes she could go shopping with me. I text her we must have a girls day out and go to lunch and shop, she agrees and says she'll talk to me later. I quickly text her again to let her know I want to take my little niece and nephews shopping as well. She responds, fasho. Coco tells me all the time that she appreciates everything I do for her and the kids. I see we are approaching Union Square. I place my phone back in my purse and wait for us to park. The subdivider's window comes down and Ben announces we've arrived at our destination. X, exits the front seat and opens my door. I step out and Ben is standing there smiling at me. I move close to him and give him a hug. "What's that for?" he asks. "I'm just giving the birthday boy a hug," I sing. His smile gets bigger; I interlock arms with him and we walk off leaving the grumpy giant behind us. The giant catches up to us and I tell them both I hope they have on their walking shoes cause we are about to do some serious damage. Ben and I walk side by side and X is right behind me. I tell Ben and X we will just do shoes and purses today and I won't put them through the agony of trying on clothes. First stop, the Gucci store. After the purchase of a 'Stirrup Medium Top Handle Bag' with matching wallet we were on our way to the Louis Vuitton store. X carries my bag and continues to follow right behind me and Ben. The Louis Vuitton store made me very happy and I purchased the Alma MM red handbag with matching wallet of course. I hand those bags to X as well. He's big and can handle it. I make my way to Neiman Marcus but for whatever reason my stomach is feeling a little queasy. On the way to Neiman's, I stop in the Cartier store and look around for a watch for Ben's birthday. I ask Ben to come with me inside to help me pick out a watch, he smiles and says, "With pleasure but we call these 'time pieces'. You purchase watches at Target." "Oh excuse me Mister, teach me. I know a hell of a lot about women's clothes, shoes, handbags, but I guess I didn't know too much about men's stuff." I tell Ben to look for a 'time piece' he likes and that would be a good gift for someone special. Ben smiles and says, "No problem." He inquires if there is a price range, I respond "no". Ben is looking around and lining up pieces he wants to take a closer look at. I take a seat as my stomach feels like it's about to explode. I ask the salesperson if there was a ladies room I could use. The salesperson points me in the direction of the ladies room and I make my way there. Ben calls, "Ms. Sydney where are you going?" "To the ladies room, I'll be right back. Keep looking for a gift for me please," I shout back. I make it to the ladies room just in time of losing my breakfast. I throw some water on my face to remove the sweat that has accumulated on my face. I retrieve a travel size tooth brush and tooth paste I always keep in my purse in case of emergency such as this one. I hear a hard knock on the door and the deep voice of X on the other side. "Ms. Sydney, is everything okay in there?" "Yes X, I'll be right out." I respond. I quickly brush my teeth and exit the ladies room to find Ben and X standing there waiting for me. "Are you okay Ms. Sydney?" Ben asks. "Yes Ben, I'm fine just a little stomachache." He has a concerned look on his face. "Maybe we should leave now," he expresses. "Yes we can leave as soon as you show me the watch, I mean 'time piece' you selected for me." He interlocks arms with me and we walk over to the counter and the salesman shows me a beautiful contemporary and refined Calibre de Cartier with a round form, white gold and a black leather band. I tell Ben it's beautiful and he agrees but expresses he would never spend seven-thousand dollars on a watch even if he had it to spend. "Don't you mean 'time piece'," I tease. Ben admires the time piece and I see a little sparkle in his eyes. I tell the salesman that this one is perfect and I will take it. I hand him the credit card and tell him it's a gift and if he wouldn't mind wrapping it for me. The salesman processes the charge card and has another salesperson wrap the gift. After my short shopping spree we head back to the car to head home because I am really not feeling well. We get back to the Fairmount and Ben is gathering my bags and hands them to X so he can carry them up to the apartment for me. Ben indicates that Phoenix has sent him a text message to come up as well. We all make it up to the apartment and when the door opens there's an aroma that hit us in the face that's so intoxicating. After entering the apartment, Phoenix and Aunt Hattie yells, "Happy Birthday Ben!" Ben is surprised by the gesture. The dining room table is set and Aunt Hattie is in the kitchen finishing up dinner. She shouts, "Dinner will be ready in 45 minutes. Have a drink and relax until it's ready." I excuse myself and retreat to the master suite. I take an antacid and quickly wash up. I will lie down for thirty minutes and rejoin the party shortly. Phoenix crawls in bed next to me and whispers to me that dinner is ready. I open my eyes to the beautiful man staring at me. "How are you feeling sweetheart?" he asks. "Much better," I respond. "Good, we're waiting for you to join us." He kisses my forehead and leaves the room. I get up and freshen up and surprisingly I feel one-hundred percent better. I grab a little something out of my purse for Phoenix, quickly changed my clothes and rejoin the party. All the guys are sitting at the bar having a drink; Aunt Hattie is setting the table and placing the food on it. Phoenix introduces me to a couple of people who have joined the party. We all sit at the table and are ready to enjoy this feast Aunt Hattie has prepared. She prepared Bake Ziti with Italian Sausage, Spinach Lasagna, Chicken Marsala, salad and garlic bread. We're sitting around the table conversing and enjoying each other's company. I look at Phoenix and he leans in and kisses me. I think this is the perfect time for a little fun. I hand him a little finger-size remote. He looks at me with a strange look on his face. He whispers in my ear, "What's this?" I smile a sinister smile and respond, "Our entertainment tonight." He smiles still with a little uncertainty, not sure what I handed him. The toy of choice tonight is a wireless bullet with ten speeds. I placed the other part of the toy, the bullet in my panties with direct contact to my clitoris. I tell Phoenix to put his arm around my chair and hit the 'On' button. The vibration radiates and he feels the intensity of the vibration and asks, "Where is this coming from?" He has a seductive smile and whispers, "Where is it baby?" "It's in my panties resting on my clit." "Ah yeah...this is going to be fun!" he responds with much enthusiasm. He leans back in his chair and has a seductive smile plastered across his face. X and the other two guests are still sitting at the table conversing about something, when Phoenix interjects and joins the conversation. I'm responding to some text messages when Phoenix hits the switch and catches me off guard and I let out a slight yelp. Everyone turns to me with a concern look on their faces but Phoenix is smiling. It's still vibrating and I'm trying to keep a straight face because this shit feels good. "Are you okay Ms. Sydney?" X asks. "Oh yes, I'm just fine. I just had a little chill that went through my body...thanks but I'm good, really good!" X turns and returns to his conversation and I look at Phoenix who is in fact enjoying this. He hits another speed and I am very close to climaxing. He can tell I'm close because it's hard to contain my facial expression; I have my eyes closed and biting my bottom lip. He puts his arm around me and whispers in my ear, "Cum on baby...cum at the table with everyone sitting here. This shit is turning me on. I'm so hard just watching you get yours baby. After you cum, we're going to the bedroom so I can make you cum some more." Oh shit, I am getting ready to cum! The hard part is not to scream out with pleasure at this table. Phoenix is sucking on my earlobe and kissing my neck which is driving me insane...fuck, I explode! Phoenix knows he got me there because he giggles in my ear and says, "That's my girl." I open my eyes and Aunt Hattie is staring right at us. She inquires, "What are you two doing?" I lower my head and Phoenix responds, "Nothing Auntie, I'm just whispering sweet nothings in her ear." "Yeah, piss on me and tell me it's raining," she responds sarcastically. Aunt Hattie starts to remove the dinner dishes from the table and X stands to assist her. Ben comes back in the dining room to assist but she tells him to have a seat, it's his birthday and he needs to relax. Once the table is cleared, Aunt Hattie brings out a beautiful birthday cake. Phoenix asks me what did I purchase today, and I told him a few handbags with matching wallets. He says, "That's all babe? I thought you were going to do some damage." "Yes, that's all. I didn't feel very well so we cut the shopping spree short." I stand and excuse myself, "I'll be right back." I went to the master suite to retrieve the watch I purchased today for Ben. He is going to have a cow knowing I had him select his own gift. I returned with the Cartier bag and placed it on the floor until after we sing 'Happy Birthday'. We all join in on the birthday song and Ben blows out his candles. Aunt Hattie hands him a box. He opens it to find, two round-trip tickets to Jamaica. Ben stands and gives her a hug and kiss on the cheek and asks, "Why the big box for an envelope?" She responds, "To throw you off." We all laugh. The other two guests present a card that contains gifts cards to Target, Best Buy, and Macys. I take the bag that I have at my side and place it on the table. Phoenix and I say at the same time, "Happy Birthday Ben!" Ben has a very surprised look on his face and says, "I can't accept this gift. It's way too expensive." Phoenix yells to Ben, "You deserve the gift, now open it so the rest of us can see." Ben unwraps the box and pulls out the timepiece that he selected earlier today. "Wow, man that's nice." Ben looks at me and calls me sneaky. "How could you have me pick out my own gift, Ms. Sydney?" He asks. "What better way to get what you want than to pick it out yourself." I expressed. Everyone laughs, eats their cake, and continues enjoying each other's company.

Chapter eighteen

I wake up with the worst stomach cramps in the world. I reach over to the nightstand to see if Phoenix has any pain killers, and he doesn't. Since there are no pain killers in the drawer, I'll have to check the medicine cabinet in the bathroom. I pull the covers from over my body and slide my house shoes on to make my way to the bathroom. I search the medicine cabinet for pain killers. I think to myself, I haven't had cramps like this in a long time. I don't have enough energy to make it to the kitchen to get bottled water so I turn on the sink faucet, pop two Tylenols in my mouth, and with my hand drink enough water to make the pills go down. I pray they take effect quickly because these cramps are kicking my butt. I head back to the bed to lie down until this passes. I fall back to sleep and then the ringing of my cell phone startles me. Still with my eyes closed I reach for my cell phone, not looking at who is calling, I answer "hello?" Amber's voice is on the other line. She is ranting and raving about how she has not talked to me and questioned me about my whereabouts. I tell her to slow down and breathe. She's talking a mile a minute. Finally she says, "Syd you don't sound good, are you sick?" "I have the worst cramps in the world, I've never had cramps like this before sis," I respond. She gets worried as she always does and tells me she will come over and check on me. She said she will just use her key so I don't have to get up to answer the door. I tell Amber "that's fine but I'm not at home." "Then where are you Sydney?" She asks in a cynical voice. "I'm at my boyfriend's house." I tell her it's not necessary to come over because it's just cramps and I will call her if it doesn't get better. I fall back to sleep and dream of

Phoenix and how much I'm enjoying being with him; how he looks at me when we make love and how he makes me laugh. I dream that we're married and we have twins; a boy and a girl. I wake up sweating to find Amber sitting at my bedside. "Sydney, are you okay honey? You were dreaming and you're sweating profusely." I gather my thoughts and try to figure out how she got in here. "I was just having a dream. How did you find me and how did you get in here?" I ask perplexed. "Don't worry about that baby sister; I'm here to take care of you." She tells me that sweating like this is not normal and wants to know how I feel right now. "I still have cramps, something's wrong. I should not have cramps for this long." Amber has a look of panic on her face and asks if I have enough energy to put some clothes on because she's taking me to urgent care. I try to remove my legs from under the covers and get so dizzy that I feel like I am going to pass out. I tell her I have a sweatsuit on the sofa to put on. She moves over to the sofa to retrieve my clothes and helps me get dressed. I tell Amber I can go in my PJ's the way I'm feeling and she sort of chuckles and says, "Babe look at yourself." I look down and all I have on is a thong and I laugh. "I guess I should put something on." She helps me slide my pants on then my jacket. My flip-flops are next to the bed, so I slid those on as well. She reminisces about when we were little and she used to help me get dressed. I tell her I'm a grown-ass woman with grown-ass parts and it's a shame right now that she is helping me put my clothes on. She laughs, and says, "I will always be your big sister and I will always be here for you." "Sis, I'm so dizzy, I don't think I can walk without falling." Amber retrieves her cell from her purse and dials a number. I hear her tell someone I'm not feeling well and she needs help getting me to her car. Within minutes, I hear the doorbell ring. Amber gets up and walks out of the bedroom to answer the door. Moments later she returns with X by her side. He picks me up and heads for the door. I don't like this man but right now I'm grateful he's here to help me. Amber grabs my purse and cell phone and all three of us walk out the door. Amber locks the door and we wait patiently for the elevator. We get downstairs and exit the double glass doors to find Ben waiting. "Ma'am, where are we taking Ms. Sydney?" "Kaiser San Francisco please," she speaks softly. We pull up to Kaiser Hospital on Geary Street in San Francisco. Amber gets out and tries to find a wheelchair. She comes to the passenger side, X opens the door, helps me out of the car and into a wheelchair. X tells Amber to go with Ben to park the car and he will wait with me. Ben and Amber pull off to find a parking space. X and I are in the aisle waiting for them to meet back up with us when we hear a car burn rubber in the parking lot. I think to myself, what asshole is driving like that in a parking structure. I look up and much to my surprise I see a black car coming in our direction. I must be tripping and paranoid because there are plenty of black four door cars with tented windows in San Francisco. I push the thought out of my mind because it's probably just a coincidence. The chance of it being the same car that's been following us for the past few weeks is slim to none. X rolls the wheelchair close to a parked car so that I'm not in the way of any passing cars. His cell phone rings and he reaches in his pocket to answer it. I think I hear Ben and Amber walking up and talking in the background. I'm feeling even weaker and really think we need to hurry up before I pass out. X is still talking on the phone when I look up and see the black four door car slowly moving in our direction. Again, I think nothing of it and try to focus on what's wrong with me. Within an instant, the black car was three parked cars away from us when it picked up speed, heading right for me. Everything around me was moving in slow motion as I tried to comprehend what was about to happen. I grab the wheels of the wheelchair and the damn thing is not moving, fuck the breaks are on. I fumble to release the breaks and remember I'm weak not crippled, I can walk, and I use the arms on the wheelchair to pull myself up so I can get the hell out the way. I freeze as the car nears me; I scream and the last thing I hear is my sister screaming my name…then darkness.

I struggle to open my eyes and it's difficult for me to speak. When my eyes finally open I'm in a room with dimmed lights and I can hear voices. "Hello?" I struggle to say. Amber appears at my side and I'm trying to figure out what the hell is going on. She tells me, "Shh Syd, don't try to speak." She squeezes my hand and there are tears in her eyes. She looks tired, like she hasn't slept in days. I swallow and try to speak anyway. My throat is sore and my lips feel like sandpaper. I'm struggling but the words are not coming out. I slightly turn my head to the left and see Phoenix and my heart drops. What the fuck is going on? I ask myself. Phoenix then replaces Amber at my bedside. He leans over the rail, grabs my hand and kisses my forehead. He then pulls up a chair to sit next to me. He looks deep into my eyes, with tears welling up in his. This must really be bad because everyone is here. I look to my right and see Ben, Rocky, Coco and X conversing in a corner. I look back at Phoenix and he tells me he loves me and that I scared him; he thought he was going to lose me. "Baby, I'm so glad you're going to be okay. I can't lose you. I can't lose anyone else that I love." Tears are rolling down my cheeks. I try to speak again but the words won't come out. Phoenix places his finger up to my lips instructing me not to speak. "You're going to be alright babe, and I will not leave your side. I need you in my life forever." He declares. It takes all the energy I have to squeeze his hand to acknowledge what he's just said. I then see Rocky stand behind Phoenix and wait patiently to have his turn at my bedside. Rocky bends over to kiss my forehead then my cheek. He stares at me for a while before he speaks, and when he does there's so much anger in his face that it frightens me. I've given up trying to speak so I just listen. He says, "Sydney, I will find this motherfucker that did this to you and I promise I will personally kill that son of a bitch if it's the last thing I do!" An Asian man in a white coat stands behind Rocky and tells him that he needs to check my vitals; I assume this is the doctor. Rocky kisses my cheek again and moves away. The man stands next to the bed looking at some contraption next to my bed with wires going in a million directions and beeping sounds making their own beat. He writes something on a pad then turns to me. "Hello, Ms. Marshall. You had a lot of people worried about you. I'm Dr. Wong and I've been caring for you for the past three weeks." WHAT THE FUCK! Did this man just say he's been caring for me for the past three weeks, I scream in my head? I try to pull myself up, a machine starts to beep and the doctor put his hand on my shoulder and tells me to please relax. I have no other choice because I have no strength to move. Dr. Wong proceeds to tell me that I was a victim of a hit-and-run accident. I hear Rocky blurt out, "She was intentionally ran over in this hospital's parking structure. Don't try to sugarcoat this shit." The doctor looks back in the direction of Rocky and tells him that if he is going to continue with these outbursts that he will need to leave because he does not want him to upset me. Rocky shouts, he's not going anywhere. The doctor said then he would like for him to relax. The doctor turns back to me and continues with his report. Dr. Wong indicates that my legs are broken and I will need a good amount of physical therapy, two ribs are fractured and I had a pretty serious head injury. He mentions he's impressed with my recovery progress and that I am a tough cookie despite my injuries. He repeats that I was placed in a medically induced coma due to the head trauma. "I'm also pleased to report that you have no brain damage and with therapy you will be up and running around in no time and completely back to normal." He looks at Phoenix and Amber and tells them to call him if they have any questions. He's walking out the door when he turns back and says, "Oh I almost forgot, congratulations! The pregnancy was not harmed by this ordeal. The last ultrasound showed two strong heartbeats and again, you will be up and running way before the babies are due. Everyone have a wonderful afternoon," he says and leaves the room. Okay I really know I have a head injury because I could have sworn he said I was pregnant with twins. Tears immediately start to flow and these are not tears of joy…they are tears of great sadness. I try to sit up once again and the machine starts to beep again. Phoenix comes to my side. Phoenix reaches over to wipe the tears from my cheeks and tells me he loves me and that everything will be fine. "I'm going to take care of you and our babies; and no one will ever hurt you again." I close my eyes and pray that when I open them again this will all be some horrible, horrible nightmare! I hear voices and I open my eyes to see the same faces in the dimly lit room but this time there was an additional man and woman talking to Phoenix and Rocky. Amber sees that I have opened my eyes and pulls her chair close to my bed. This time I try to pull myself up and no machines beep. I notice I only had an IV in my arm which doesn't prevent me from sitting up in the bed. I sit up and look at everyone in the room trying to figure out what is going on. Phoenix looks at me, smiles and says, "Well hello sleeping beauty. How do you feel?" I open my mouth and the words actually come out, "Better. I'm a little stiff and somewhat in pain," I reply. He moves close to the other side of the bed and leans in to kiss me but I turn my face. He looks surprised. "I'm sorry, but I'm sure it's been a very long time since I've brushed my teeth. I'm sure it smells like someone died in my mouth." Rocky laughs and shouts, "She's back!" The man and woman come close to the bed and introduce themselves as Detectives Watson and Kendrick. Detective Watson said, "Ms. Marshall we had the pleasure of meeting a while back when you and your sister came down to the station to file a report; this is my partner and we've been assigned to your case." Detective Kendrick asks if I am up for answering some questions. "Sure," I reply. Detective Kendrick then pulls a black pad and pen out of the inside pocket of his suit jacket to jot down some notes. "Can you tell me what you remember about that day Ms. Marshall? Please start from the beginning; no detail is too small and can be very important," he instructs. I close my eyes and try to remember the events of that day. I tell the detectives that I remember my sister coming over to Phoenix's apartment because I didn't feel well and she wanted to take me to urgent care. We left the apartment and were in the parking lot of the hospital and she tried to find me a wheelchair because I was too weak to walk. After she found the wheelchair she and X helped me in. X was on the phone and Ben and Amber went to park the car. "I shouldn't have left her," Amber says through tears. I then tell the detectives I heard a car's tires screeching through the parking lot and wondered why someone was driving fast like that in a hospital parking lot. I tell them I remembered seeing a black four door car moving slowly in my direction. Phoenix chimes in and informs the detectives that someone has been following me for weeks now. Detective Kendrick writes down what Phoenix just told him and looks at me and asks me to continue. "X moved me close to the parked cars so I would not be in the way of passing cars. The next thing I knew, this car was coming straight towards me and I heard my sister scream, that's all I can remember." Detective Watson tells me that's wonderful and that I have been very helpful. I ask the detectives if they had any other information, did they know who did this to me. Detective Kendrick announced that they were following up on some leads and that they have reviewed the parking lot security footage and what they saw was what I just told them and that it was a black sedan with dark tented windows with no license plates on the front or the back of the car. "Don't worry Ms. Marshall; we will catch the son of a bitch that did this to you," says Detective Watson; the other detective looks at Watson and told her to chill out and watch her mouth. "Do you have any enemies that would want to hurt you that you can think of," asks Detective Watson. "I can only think of one person." Detective Watson says, "I know exactly who you are talking about and trust me we have already interrogated Cameron. He had a solid alibi as to his whereabouts at the time of the crime, so we had to rule him out for now. I truly believe his alibi is covering for him and he had something to do with your hit-and-run and attempted murder." A cold chill ran through my body, could Cameron really be capable of trying to kill me? I answer myself...yes. He tried it once, what makes me think he wouldn't try it again. I remember like it was yesterday when he choked me and the look on his face was like the devil himself showed his face to me and I believed him when he said if he couldn't have me then no one could. I guess he was tired of threatening me and was ready to cash in on his promise. Detective Kendrick indicates that they are keeping a watch on him but right now they have no supporting evidence that he is the one behind the act. The detective also said that he took statements from Rocky and Ben and they are also reviewing security tapes from the club's parking lot and the tapes from the hotel's security system. After a few more questions, the detectives wished me well and a speedy recovery. They will check back with me if anything changes with the investigation. There was a brief silence in the room when Phoenix spoke and asks Amber and Rocky if they would oppose of him speaking to me alone for a few moments. Neither one of them had a problem with me and Phoenix being alone. Amber comes over and kisses my forehead and she and Rocky exit the room. Phoenix pulls up a chair and grabs my hand. He stares at me with nothing but love, pain, hurt, and anger in his eyes. He didn't speak for a while, we just look at each other and again tears well up in my eyes. I ask him to tell me the truth, "Will I be able to walk again?" His voice was raspy, maybe a little hoarse but he replies with a simple, "Yes, baby you will." He told me that I can wiggle my toes and all the tests and x-rays indicate that the breaks in my legs were clean with no shattered bones which make them easier to heal. Don't worry about that now, you will have plenty time to recover," he expresses. He explains to me how Amber got his number from Rocky and needed to know how to get to me. So, he authorized the front desk to provide her with a key and that she had Ben and X at her disposal. "Ben called me to let me know they were taking you to the hospital and I left the office and arrived at the hospital minutes after the accident. This is when I met your sister babe. I thought you had tough skin, but you and your sister are truly cut from the same cloth. Because Amber didn't know me, I had no say as far as your treatment was concerned. Over the past few weeks, she and I have become close because we have one thing in common, we both love you. I was very forward and stern with her and let her know that she is in charge but I am madly in love with you and I will not leave your side. I wanted to make sure you were getting the best treatment possible. Amber let it be known that she was well aware of how to take care of her baby sister. I had to respect her wishes but she respected mine and knew I was not leaving your side," he explains.

Chapter nineteen

Phoenix told me that he had to concede and sit back and let Amber do what she does best, take care of me. "I think she understands that I am not some fly by night dude in your life. I explained to her that we have only known each other for a short while but I fell in love with you the moment I laid eyes on you. She laughed and said, "Sydney has that effect on men." I told her I was well aware of your profession and support you one-hundred percent. I also told her that you felt the same way about me, and you would show it in due time." I smiled and thanked him for being by my side and for not putting up a fight with my sister. Phoenix indicates that Amber softened up a little after the doctor came back with the preliminary findings and my blood test results. Phoenix was going over the events of how everything played out. He explains how Dr. Wong came in and hung x-rays on the monitor and explained the breaks in my legs, my fractured ribs and how my recovery would play out. "Amber, Rocky and I had so many questions that I felt sorry for the doctor," he said. His eyes lit up and he says, "We were all relieved that you didn't have any life-threatening injuries and knew we would all be a part of your recovery, but we were all blown away when he reported that your recovery should not affect the progress of your pregnancy." Phoenix said the room went completely silent and the doctor looked like he said something wrong, then realized the news of the pregnancy was a shock to everyone. The doctor apologized for the shocking news, said congratulations and that an Ob/Gyn would be in to check me out. I lay there with my mouth wide open still in shock myself. Phoenix squeezes my hand and proceeds with his story. He tells me "Amber did not want just any OB doctor checking you out, that she would call your personal doctor, who knew your history to come examine you." Phoenix then tells me Dr. Allen came to visit me the very next day and gave me a full examination. Amber and I have been seeing Dr. Allen for years and she is all too familiar with both of our medical histories. Dr. Allen has treated me for cysts, fibroids, irregular period, etc., and she has been helping Amber with trying to get pregnant for years. She is more like a sister to us than our doctor, that's why I'm sure Amber was so adamant about having her tend to my medical needs. Phoenix then tells me when Dr. Allen came to visit she performed more tests and confirmed I was in fact pregnant and that my FSH levels were very high and she wanted to do some follow-up tests as well as an ultrasound. She wanted to wait a few weeks to see if the blood test levels would change and if they didn't she would discuss the outcome. He explains "the levels did not change and when she came back to perform the ultrasound Amber and I saw some images that she pointed out and heard what sounded like thumping sounds under water. Dr. Allen confirmed her findings that there were two amniotic sacs and she heard two very strong heartbeats. Phoenix tells me he and Amber exchanged words as to him being the father and how was she to know that since her sister was in a coma. Dr. Allen offered to perform a DNA/paternity test on the blood she had already taken on me to put Amber's mind at ease and Phoenix agreed. Of course the results confirmed that Phoenix was 99.9 % the father. After they were given the results, Amber was a little nicer but he noticed Rocky became distant, he explained.

Phoenix tells me he knows this is a lot to take in and that it will take some time getting used to. I reply, "To say the least." This is truly too much for me and I tell Phoenix I think I need to sleep. He stands to move to a recliner and tells me to get some rest and that he will be right here when I awake. Before I close my eyes, I give Phoenix a caring look and tell him, "I believe I have fallen in love with you. This is unfamiliar territory for me and I am open to venture in this love game because you have proven to be an amazing man, in the short time we've known each other. I'm not sure how this will work out but I will be optimistic and give us a chance." Before I knew it, tears are rolling down my face and I tell him that I don't know what kind of mother I'll be and that it's difficult for me to fathom the thought of being someone's mother and being responsible for their lives. A lot has happened from me meeting him, to falling in love, then getting hit by a car to being pregnant with twins...this is enough to drive anyone crazy and if my legs weren't broke that I'd run away. He consoles me and lets me know that he loves me and that he is here and will be with me all the way and that we will get through this together. He leans and kisses me on the forehead, my cheeks, my chin, and then lastly my lips. His lips are so soft and the feeling I get when he touches me is indescribable. In an instant all my cares drift away and I feel confident that he is sincere and will do as he says. He tells me that I will be a fantastic mother and he wants nothing more than to be a father for our children and to make me the happiest woman in the world. I guess he believes in fairytales, I think to myself. I'm sure he wants to give his children the same love and care that his parents gave him. I interrupt him and say, "You had the classic example of what love really is. Therefore, you have that to pass along to your children. I didn't have that so I'm not sure I can give them the love they will need and deserve," I conveyed. "My parents were far from role models, hell I'm far from a role model, to think, a woman who takes off her clothes for money trying to be someone's mother just doesn't seem right Phoenix," I cried. "Baby you are so hard on yourself, you are beautiful, smart, funny, and caring, you have plenty to offer our children and you will not be doing this by yourself. I will be with you every step of the way and you have no idea how excited your sister is about you being pregnant. "Speaking of twins, you made several references about twins, how ironic it is that I'm carrying your babies," I ask. He laughs and says he's always wanted twins, a boy and a girl and wanted it to be with the woman he fell madly in love with. Phoenix seemed sad and expressed that he and his sister, Montana, were very close and inseparable and that he would want the same for his children. This is the first time he's mentioned his sister and I want to know more about her but I don't want to press the issue. He told me that his parents and sister were his life and when they were killed he felt like his world had been shattered in a million pieces. He could not survive another loss and prayed that God would fill his life with a caring and loving wife and two children. Maybe he felt like God owed him because *HE* took the only people in the world he loved, I thought. I'm happy half of his prayer was answered…two children. I pray now that I can make him happy! Phoenix got quiet again then spoke, "I believe everything happens for a reason, either for good or bad, people are placed in your life for whatever reason and if it weren't for Ben, I would not be sitting next to the woman of my dreams. I will forever be grateful to him," he cries. I reached up to wipe his tears away as my waterfalls was streaming down my face, he kisses me passionately and our kiss is interrupted with the clearing of Amber's throat as she and Rocky re-enter my hospital room. Amber says, "Uh hello Mr. Davenport. I would love to spend some time with my sister if you don't mind." "Of course Amber. I'll go grab something to eat babe and I'll be back." He kisses me on the lips and heads for the exit. Before walking out the door, he asks if Amber or Rocky needed anything and they both say no thanks at the same time. Rocky looks in my direction and nods his head "hello"; I smile and nod back. He then takes a chair in the corner and pulls out his cell phone. Amber puts her purse and the bags she's carrying on the counter next to the sink and came and sat next to me in the very small hospital bed. She touches my hand and starts to cry. "Amber, what's wrong babe?" I ask. "Syd, I was so scared. I thought you wouldn't come out of the coma and if I lost you, I would die," she cries. I tell her to stop crying because as she can see, I'm fine and my injuries are not life-threatening. Amber says through tears that she blames herself for the car hitting me because she should have never went with Ben to park the car. She indicates she should have stayed with me and took me directly in urgent care after I got in the wheelchair. "I should have followed my first mind, and maybe that maniac would not have tried to kill you," she cries. I grab Amber's hand and tell her this is in no way her fault and neither one of us could have known something like this would or could have happened. She says, "I know Syd, but I was not able to protect you as I always have." I tell Amber to please don't blame herself and try to get past this and look forward to the future. She starts to cry even more for some reason. She gently rests her head on my shoulder and takes her hand and rubs it in a circular motion on my stomach. "These are tears of joy because you are carrying my niece and nephew for us to love." I say, "Oh Lord, Phoenix has you thinking girl and boy as well?" She sniffs, wipes her nose and eyes and replies, "Yes, we have already named them." I laugh and say, "We don't even know what they are; it's too early to find out." "You're right but you can't blame us for wishful thinking," she says. All of a sudden Rocky gets up and walks out the room without saying anything. Amber and I look back at each other and shrug our shoulders. Amber continues to tell me that the boy's name will be Phoenix after him and his father and the girl will be named Brooklyn. "If we have a girl I think we should name her Montana, after his sister." Amber burst out with laughter and it kind of startles me out of my thoughts, and says, "I hope the kids don't get teased because they're named after a city and state," she sings. I tell her it would mean a lot to him if we named our daughter after his sister. Amber agreed. All of a sudden Amber's happiness turned to sadness. She states, "I'm super excited sis that you are pregnant and I'm glad we are going to be able to share something I've wanted for many years, a child. Since having my own doesn't seem to be in the cards, I will have to live vicariously through you." This girl is like Dr. Jekyll and Mr. Hyde because she goes from one extreme to the next. I understand why she's sad because she has been trying to get pregnant but for some reason it's just not happening. Dr. Allen has done a number of tests that indicate she's healthy and her husband's sperm has been checked and he's fine. It's just one of those things that no one can explain. "Trust me sis, this was not planned. You know how I feel about responsibility for others. If it were up to me, I'd give you both of them to raise." I say. I didn't mention to Amber about Phoenix because I didn't know where this whole thing with him was going and she knows I don't fall for guys or get serious with them. I wanted to tell her I was experiencing something with feelings that I had never felt before. But talking to Amber sometimes is like being in a therapy session because she has to analyze the entire conversation and sometimes I just need her to listen. I express that "Phoenix is smart, handsome, successful, kind, funny, and just an overall nice guy who seems to have fallen in love with me and it feels good to have someone like that in your life." She's quiet for a moment and staring at me like she's looking for the right words. I think, oh dear here we go, what is she thinking or going to say. I brace myself for the worst. She speaks and says, "Phoenix seems like a nice guy, we got to know each other since you've been in the hospital and I would have to say that I like this guy and I feel he's good for you sis. He cares and loves you and he has proved that when he tried to tell me what was best for you. I almost had his ass kicked out the hospital because he was 'stranger danger'," she laughs. "But I'm guessing you must have feelings for this man since you had sex with him without protection." I knew it was coming. "He's fine Amber. I've seen his blood results and he's negative for all sexually transmitted diseases." "Well that's good to hear but I already knew because I had him tested." "Excuse me!" I shout. "How in the hell did you have him tested?" I questioned. She proceeds to tell me when I was in the coma she wanted to make sure he was the father and had Dr. Allen do a paternity test. "While she was doing that, I also asked her to do an HIV and other disease tests since she already had his blood." "That had to be against the law," I state. "Maybe, but you were in no position to confirm so I did what I thought was best under the circumstances," she responds with authority. I communicated that what's done is done and we need to move on. I thank her for all of her support and for being by my side. She tells me things happen for a reason and maybe meeting Phoenix and getting pregnant was God's way of slowing me down and taking me from the fast life I'm living. I smile and think; okay we'll go with that. We continue to laugh and talk about Phoenix. I tell her that I really like Phoenix and he is not like any other guy I've been involved with. "I think I could say I love him." "He's sweet and he's really into me and just not in the physical sense but he inspires me to be me and to do whatever I want to do that makes me happy. He's told me that he wants to be with me for the rest of his life." "Sydney, I think you have really found the one, I have never heard you speak this way about any man before. I believe that's a sure sign that Phoenix is true and he will be true to you," she says. "I hope so Amber, I'm apprehensive because every time I get close to someone it never works out, it always ends in heartbreak or tragedy and I can't take any more heartbreak, heartache, or tragedy in my life." Amber tells me she knows all too well about the heartbreak and tragedy but look what happened to her. She let down her wall and fell madly in love with an amazing man and she knows I can find the same in Phoenix. "Speaking of amazing man, I need to go home to my husband," she says, stands, kisses me on the forehead and tells me she will see me tomorrow. Shortly after Amber leaves, Phoenix and Dr. Wong enter the room holding a conversation like they've known each other forever. Dr. Wong tells me that my recovery has been wonderful and he will release me from the hospital tomorrow. He also lets me know that the discharge nurse will come in to give me all the instructions for getting started with my physical therapy and follow-up appointments. He wishes me well and tells me not to hesitate to call him if I have any questions, concerns, or pain. Dr. Wong shakes Phoenix's hand and tells him to take good care of me. Phoenix replies, "Don't worry, I have all intentions to do just that." Dr. Wong leaves the room and before the door closes, in walks Rocky. He states he is going to meet up with Ben to check on the boys and says he will be here in the morning when I'm released. I blow him a kiss and tell him to kiss my babies for me and tell them I miss them. He laughs and says, "I really believe they miss you too. I'll leave you two lovebirds alone." He blows me a kiss, tells us good night and leaves. Rocky doesn't seem like his jolly self, once I get home I will call him so we can spend some quality time alone. I understand that Phoenix has not left my side since I've been here so it's hard for anyone else to get time in. Phoenix has dinner ordered for us, and we sit in my hospital room with candles lit enjoying each other's company waiting for our dinner to be delivered. I lay in the hospital bed and he is next to me in the recliner. Once the food arrives, we enjoy prime rib, Maine Lobster, garlic potatoes, green salad, mixed vegetables and rolls. I have no idea why Phoenix ordered so much food; it was enough to feed a small army. When the nurse came in to check on me, Phoenix offers her a plate and she gladly accepts. Soon a few more staff members came trickling in to see if there was any food left so they didn't have to eat the stale food from the hospital's cafeteria. Dinner was amazing, the both of us are full and Phoenix squeezes in the bed next to me and we attempt to watch a Criminal Minds marathon on TV. We are both wakened by a nurse who needs to check my vitals. She apologizes for waking us up and said she knows it's early but she needs to get my vitals so I can stay on track to leave later on in the day. She takes my blood pressure, temperature, and pulse, writes it all down on her clipboard then apologizes again for the early morning interruption and leaves the room. Phoenix and I nestle back together and shortly fall back to sleep.

Chapter twenty

We were awakened again at 7:00am at the next nurse shift change. This time the nurse who came in introduces herself as Sharron and says she will be helping me get ready for discharge. I wanted to jump up and down and if I could have, I would have turned flips down the hallway. I can't wait to get out of this smelly place and back in the comfort of my own home. Before I leave I have to be cleared and released by all my doctors. Dr. Allen did a vaginal exam and ultrasound and said that I was good to go and she would see me in four weeks. Phoenix gathers all my stuff and we are waiting for the orderly to come with a wheelchair when the private phone rang in my room. Phoenix walks over and answers, "Hello?" he says it a few times before hanging up. He continues what he was doing when the phone rings again. Phoenix walks over to the phone and answers it once again. He says "hello" but there's no one on the other end so he hangs up. He chuckles a bit and I ask, "What's so funny?" He says, "I guess your boyfriend doesn't want to talk to me because as soon as I answer, he hangs up." I return the chuckle and say, "That might be hard since my boyfriend is in the same room with me." Phoenix plasters the biggest smile on his face and walks over to me, kisses me and gives me a big hug. "That's what I want to hear, you do like me," he laughs. "Don't push your luck mister, I can change my mind," I laugh. I tell Phoenix to not push his luck. Seconds later, Sharron the nurse, walks in my hospital room holding a large bouquet of red long stem roses. Phoenix instructs the nurse to place the flowers on the counter with the other flower arrangements and cards that I've received over the past weeks. I turn and notice a card sticking out of the arrangement and ask Phoenix to grab the card for me please. He removes the card and hands it to me; I open the little envelope to read the contents. My heart sinks when I see the words on the card; it reads:

I hope you're feeling better Ms. Sydney Marshall,

But it doesn't matter because your soul belongs to me!

See you in HELL bitch!

Phoenix sees the horror on my face and takes the card from my still hands. He says out loud, "That's it; I'm tired of this bullshit." He pulls out his cell phone and dials a number. Phoenix starts to talk and I realize he's speaking to one of the detectives, his last words before he hangs up his phone were, "I expect for you and your partner to handle this or I will take matters in my own hands." Phoenix is clearly upset and tells me that I cannot go back to my place because it's not safe. I tell Phoenix that nobody is going to run me out of my own home and I want to go to my apartment. He tries to plead with me about going back. He tells me he will send X to pick up anything I need including the dogs. I'm flattered with his gesture, but I would like to go to my apartment and get my own things. "Babe it is very clear that someone is trying to harm you and I will not allow it. Please don't fight me on this, just let me take care of you." He pleads. I try and stand but I'm quickly reminded that I need assistance. It will be a few more months before I can stand on my own two feet, literally. I ask Phoenix if we can make a deal. "I am a reasonable person babe as long as it will not cause you any additional harm," he responds. "No, this will not bring any more pain. I just want to swing by my place to get my own stuff and I will spend a few days at your place then I need for you to spend some time at mine." I explain. Phoenix was fine with this arrangement and will let the physical therapist know she needs to be available for both locations. There was a knock at the door. Phoenix tells whoever's knocking to come in. X walks in the room with the orderly and the wheelchair. X grabs my bags from Phoenix and he helps me into the wheelchair. Phoenix ordered a personal wheelchair for me when I leave here so I can get around during my recovery. The car is packed up, Phoenix and I are in the backseat and where're headed to my place first. We ride over to my place in complete silence and I'm trying to figure out who in the hell is trying to hurt me. For the life of me I can't figure it out. My life sure has changed and has been turned upside down, I think to myself. I can't believe I have met this wonderful man and his babies are growing inside me. This is all too good to be true, nothing good ever happens to me; there is always drama and tragedy in my life. I'm trying to stay positive so I will erase these negative thoughts out of my head because everything about Phoenix is positive and I truly believe he loves me and I love him. Everything about him is real and he has no problem expressing his love for me. We make it to my apartment building and Stanley is so excited to see me, and I was just as excited to see him. He tells me he's missed me a lot and that he and his family were praying for my recovery. I gave Stanley a big hug and a kiss on the cheek and told him I really appreciate all of his prayers. Phoenix, X, and I make it to my apartment and I was so excited to see Snickers and Teddy. Rocky was kicking it on the couch watching TV when we enter the apartment. I'm helped on the couch so I can play with the boys. I play with them for what seems like hours. After I have my quality time with my boys, I'm back in my wheelchair and slowly make my way to the bedroom to pack some things to take to Phoenix's place. Rocky follows me to the bedroom and sits on my bed. I turn to look at him as he still displays that look on his face I can't place. I'm not sure what's wrong with Rocky but his attitude has been really foul lately and I've been waiting to talk to him about it. I ask him how he's been and he tells me he was fine and I need to focus on me and not to worry about him. I tell him okay, feeling really frustrated by his attitude. I wheel myself next to him by my bed and ask him, "What the hell is your problem?" Rocky looks at me like I'm crazy and says, "I don't have a damn problem." "Rocky this is what I'm talking about. You're snapping back at me like you're mad at me or something," I express. He's so short with me, and now he's giving me major attitude and I just need to know what I've done to make him act this way with me. Rocky tells me, "Sydney it's all good, I don't have no beef with you sis." "It's funny because your actions towards me show something completely different," I express. I explain, he's not the same with me, and I always feel he's angry with me and we don't talk anymore. Rocky conveys that I don't have time for him since this Phoenix thing kicked off. "Oh is that what this is about, me and Phoenix?" I ask. Rocky frowns his face and shouts, "Hell no, not at all!" "There's really no reason to shout Rocky, we're just talking," I respond. I think I hit a nerve. He tells me he's feeling pushed out and replaced by Phoenix and his people and he's out of the loop. He indicates that he's scared and upset that someone has hurt me and feels that if he were there none of this would have happened and he blames Phoenix. I tell him that he is my brother and he can never be pushed out or replaced. I also tell him that I will talk with Phoenix and that he needs to include him in whatever decisions are being made on my behalf. He smiles and says, "I'd like that sis. I just want to make sure you are happy and safe." Rocky changes the subject and starts a conversation about Delaney. He communicates that Delaney has some family issues he needs to tend to and will be out of the country for several months and he wants us to run the business until he returns. "Since your accident I'm not sure you will be up for it, so maybe it's best to just focus on the business side and not the dancing," he says. I laugh and say, "Ya think?" He returns the laugh. I tell Rocky, "I can keep myself busy at the club and this is just what I need to keep my mind off the things that are happening in my life." I tell him he's right and since I won't be able to dance for a while I can handle the girls, the books and anything else he needs help with. Rocky confirms that this is exactly what Delaney said and that if I was not up for it he should contact him to let him know because he would just hire an accountant to come in and handle the books until he returns to the states. We discuss the club's business a little while longer and out of nowhere Rocky then tells me that if I'm not happy about the pregnancy he will take me to get an abortion and that I should not feel pressured about having a child or children if I didn't want to. I was shocked as hell and I asked him why he would say such a thing. He replies, "Sydney, between you and I, we know you are not the mother type." Again, I was shocked as hell. Yes, I thought it and even felt it when I first found out but what gives him the right to say some foul ass shit like this. I look at Rocky and tell him, "Okay I know you are obviously going through something and it is clear that it has something to do with me, but right now you are being down right mean and you're hurting my feelings." Rocky looks at me with no emotion on his face, and this does not sit right with me. "Rocky, what the fuck is wrong with you? Why are you acting so fucking mean and heartless?" I shout, obviously angry now. There's nothing…but a smug ass look on his face. He grabs my hand and says, "I'm just looking out for your best interest." "Rocky, I don't think looking out for my best interest is telling me you will take me to get an abortion and kill the two lives that are growing inside me?" He simply replies, "Sure it is." WOW, I'm completely at a loss for words and cannot understand why Rocky has taken on this 'I don't give a shit' attitude about everything including me. My life has changed drastically in the past few months, some good and some bad but mostly good. Rocky has always been in my corner, he's always had my back, no matter what, so it is really hard for me to accept his recent behavior. I look to Rocky as another brother, I love him and I appreciate all he has done for me and I mostly appreciate our friendship and the love we have for each other. But right now, I feel like he's a stranger and my heart is broken that he is treating me this way. Is it because he might be jealous of the relationship that is developing between me and Phoenix? I question myself. Could it be that Delaney left both of us in charge of the club? I'm not sure but it's heartbreaking that he is acting like this. Rocky has had my back, and saved my life from Cameron when he was choking me, he's protected me from the creeps at the club, and he's been a part of my family forever, I mean he's my brother's best friend and he promised my brother that he will watch over me, protect me, until his return and I truly believe he has done that so it's hard to understand where all this negativity is coming from. The only thing I can come up with is that he's jealous, but it's not like I haven't been with other men. Maybe this is so different because he can tell I've fallen for this guy. Again, I'm not sure what his deal is and we've never had a problem before, so I am truly stunned by his actions. I think it may be a combination of him not being included and me really digging Phoenix. I believe in my heart that when Rocky is ready to talk to me he will. I also tell him that I think Cameron is the one behind all this nonsense that's going on. He says he wouldn't put it past him and he would follow up with the detectives. I finish packing my bags and Phoenix, X and I head to Phoenix's place. I leave Rocky with the dogs at my place and tell him to call me in a few days so we can go take care of the business at the club. I feel a little down on the ride over to the Fairmount when Phoenix asks what's wrong. I tell him about the conversation Rocky and I had and how he feels left out and is being replaced. Phoenix apologized and tells me that Rocky will be included in any decisions regarding my safety. Phoenix tells me not to worry, that Rocky really loves me and is concerned about my well-being so it's understandable he feels the way he does. Phoenix also informs me that he and Rocky have bonded over the past weeks and he totally knows that Rocky is worried about me and wants the SOB that hurt me put behind bars so that he cannot hurt me again. "Rocky told me that he's upset with himself, because he was not there to protect you, and that he feels in his soul that Cameron hurt you or hired someone to hurt you and if it's the last thing on this earth he did, he was going to prove Cameron was behind this and take care of him for good," he states. Phoenix tells me it took some convincing, but Rocky promised he would let the police do their job and prove that Cameron was in fact behind these heartless acts! Rocky's a hothead, I hope he takes heave to what Phoenix said and lets the police do their jobs, somehow I don't think it's going to play out that way because he's never liked Cameron. Phoenix places his arm around me and pulls me close to him. I could feel his warm breath against my neck which makes me hot as hell. I tell him to please don't touch me because it will make me want him. Phoenix smiles at me and tells me how much he loves me and tells me not to worry that we will have the rest of our lives to make love and his main focus is for me to get well. I respond by saying, "I will get well but in the meantime I am horny as hell and need to be taken care of." Phoenix leans in and rests his forehead on mine then kisses me which send chills throughout my body and whatever feelings of hesitation about how I feel about him have just exited my body and I will completely let myself fall in love with this man. After our passionate kiss, he whispers, "I got you boo." When we enter his apartment, my second residence for a while, I was super surprised to see that Phoenix has made one of the rooms into my rehabilitation work station. I turn to him and tell him "thank you so much baby for going through all of this to make sure I'm taken care of and comfortable." He indicates he wants me to rest and when I'm ready to start its right at my fingertips. "I will rest over the weekend then I'd like to start on

Monday," I tell him. He also informs me that he has hired a full-time nurse to assist in my rehabilitation process to make sure that we are not doing anything that will harm me or the babies. Again, I feel so much love from this man I can't stand it. I call Rocky and make arrangements for us to meet to discuss our plans for the club. I reach the club Wednesday mid-afternoon and Rocky is already here and working, he is at the bar signing an invoice for the alcohol delivery that has just arrived. He looks in the direction of the front door when it opens to see who is entering the club. The sunlight from the outdoors temporarily blinds him and he has to squint his eyes to focus and see who just came in; the door closes allowing him to see me. He smiles and motions for me to meet him at the bar. Ben wheels me in the direction of the bar and I am greeted by a number of club employees who have obviously missed me. I stop and exchange some hugs and kisses and answer a few questions. X is directly behind me making sure no one gets out of control or makes any sudden moves. X tells me that everyone is a suspect until the bastard is caught. I look behind me and tell X its okay, these people are like my family and he can relax. He shakes his head and says, "I'm in control of this situation and it's my job to protect you and that is what I intend on doing." "Just don't get distracted by a phone call again," I respond sarcastically. I wheel myself the rest of the way to the bar. Rocky bends down to hug and kiss me and tells me to hang on a minute so he could finish this business and we can sit and discuss the other business at hand. Rocky and I finally sit at a table near the bar to discuss how we are going to hold down the fort while Delaney is gone. I tell Rocky that I've spoken with Delaney and he gave me instructions on how he wanted things done during his absence. Rocky immediately gets an attitude, and says he has already talked to Delaney and was given instructions as well. I now sense that Rocky is agitated and ask him what's the deal with him lately? Rocky simply replies, "Let's focus on how to handle this business and the rest is not important right now." He then says that he can have somewhat of a break since I'm not dancing and he doesn't have to watch my every move here. "Okay Roc, I feel this is personal now because you are straight shooting at me!" I scream. "What did I do to you for you to treat me like this," I ask now with tears in my eyes. "You did absolutely nothing," he replies dryly. "Then why do I detect this major attitude with you?" I question. "Look Sydney, I have a lot going on in my life right now. It's all good and I'm sorry if I've taken my frustrations out on you," he states. I still don't believe him and he's telling me this to shut me up. Okay I will let it go and hope that he will come to me when he's ready to talk. "Rocky, you're my brother and I'm here for you so whenever you're ready to talk, you let me know," I express. "Will do," was his response.

Chapter twenty-one

Rocky and I agree to get back to business. I feel I'm not getting anywhere with him regarding his recent mood swings, so I let it go. He and I spend the next two hours going over the details on how we would proceed with the business for Delaney. We agreed on all aspects and I even had Rocky laughing but then he flips back to his weird attitude when my cell phone rings and I answer, "hello babe." I'm just going to chalk this weird behavior off as something he's going through as he says and hopefully he will let me know what's going on when he's ready. Friday night will be the big test regarding running the business which I think the both of us can do with our eyes closed and I'm am not worried at all. It will be a little strange to be in the club, working pre-se, but not working the pole. In my current condition, it will be a long time before I will be able to work the pole which I so love to do. Dancing, working the pole, working the crowd, lap dances, and all other aspects of this atmosphere allows me to be in control, to call the shots, to have the power to make men do whatever I want them to do. It's a wonderful feeling. I'm not going to dwell on the past; I am going to focus on the future because I have so many wonderful people who love and care for me that I should move on and make room in my heart to accept the love that has been given to me. My cell phone rings bringing me out of my thoughts, the call is from a blocked number and I hesitate to answer with all that's going on, but I can't live my life scared and running from whoever is trying to hurt me. I'm in the club with Rocky and X and I completely feel safe so I answer the phone. I repeat "hello" a few times before I get ready to hang up the phone because the idiot on the other end is not saying anything. I move my finger to click the button to disconnect the call when I hear someone on the other end clear their voice. I say "hello" again, then I hear a familiar voice. "Sydney, I wanted to call you to see how you are doing. I heard about your accident and I am worried about you," Cameron says. "Cameron, forgive me if I don't believe you since you tried to kill me once and to tell you the truth I think you tried to kill me again and you almost succeeded!" I shout. Cameron tells me that he loves me and that he has never loved a woman like he loves me. He was angry with the break-up and his emotions got the best of him. He was upset but he would never intentionally harm me. "But you did Cameron, and to tell you the truth I'm terrified of you because I have seen firsthand what you are capable of." In a calm relaxed voice, Cameron tries to plead his case by saying he told me that if he couldn't have me no one could because he was hurt and he was trying to scare me; that no woman has ever made him feel the way I did; and he was afraid of losing me. He says when I ended things between us, he lost it and wigged out. He reports he's been getting help with his anger issues and he now realizes how he messed up and he wants to apologize for all the hurt and harm he caused me. "I accept your apology Cameron and before it gets out, I want you to know that I'm pregnant and I'm happy with my life." There's a slight hesitation then he says he is trying to move on as well and that he wants to meet me at the club so that he can put closure to our relationship and he will finally be able to move on if he sees me one last time. "Cameron, I really don't think that's necessary nor do I think it's a good idea especially since I have a restraining order against you,"

I remind him. "Oh yeah, you did take out a restraining order on me didn't you?" His voice changes from clam to irritated. The old Cameron is back, he needs to stay in anger management sessions because he's not there yet. I truly believe he suffers from Bi-Polar Disease! He indicates that because of me the media follows him around making him out to be some kind of monster; he tells me that I have ruined his image and now wherever he goes people stare and are always whispering and it makes him feel uncomfortable that I have caused the public to treat him this way. I ask Cameron does he really believe that this was all my doing. He angrily shouts, "Yes!" This man is more delusional than I thought! "Cameron I'm going to end this call now." He yells in the receiver, "This fucking phone call will end when I fucking end it! Do you understand me Sydney?" He continues to yell that he gave me everything and anything I wanted, took very good care of me and this is the way I repay him. "I don't owe you a damn thing and you have lost your fucking mind. You need to continue getting some help because you clearly still have some issues to work out!" I scream. I also tell him that it would be in his best interest not to show up at the club and to never call me again. Cameron laughs this wicked laugh and says, "You have two broken legs and fractured ribs Sydney. Just what do you think you can do to stop me, you can't even run now can you?" Okay now this nut is scaring me because how does he know about my injuries, I ask myself. He then tells me it would be such a shame if I had another accident and somehow lost my life or the life of the children I am carrying inside me. My heart drops and I don't say anything else I just click the off button and disconnect the call. I'm so upset that I am sick to my stomach and I'm searching for Rocky to let him know I'm going home. I pass X and tell him I will be ready to leave in about 5 minutes, he nods acknowledging my request. I locate Rocky, give him a hug and tell him I will see him on Friday. I then text Ben to let him know we are coming out and I was ready to go home. X wheels me out and Ben is waiting to take us home.

We get to Phoenix's place and we are hit with the smell of something cooking. Aunt Hattie is in the kitchen moving about doing what she does best, cooking. I let her know I was there and she wipes her hands on her apron that was tied around her petite waist and hurries to hug me. Aunt Hattie gives me a hug and kiss on my cheek. She has tears in her eyes. "I'm so glad you are alright my dear," she cries. She tells me that she was scared and she couldn't contain her sadness if anything happened to me. I smile and let her know I was okay and the babies are okay as well. She hugs me again, places her hand on my belly and tells me how excited she is that Phoenix and I are going to give her babies; she then returns to the kitchen to finish what she was doing. As she's walking back to the kitchen, I yell after her that I am just as excited. I ask her Phoenix's whereabouts and she points down the hall and says, "In his study." I tell her thanks and start wheeling myself down the hall. She laughs and says, "Don't let none of that hanky panky go on like you two did a couple of months back," I laugh and reply, "Okay." I reach his study and gently knock on the door that was slightly ajar, Phoenix says, 'Come in." I enter and he is sitting at his desk with his feet propped up on his desk and his arms folded behind his head. He smiles when he sees it's me and removes his feet from the desk and opens his arms for me to come to him. I head in his direction and admire how sexy he is, with his crisp white socks, faded blue jeans, and a white polo shirt on. He picks me up and sits me on his lap were I am straddling him. He wraps his arms around my neck, stares into my eyes, and kisses me deeply. We sit and chat for a while and I tell him I'm tired and would like to shower and take a nap before dinner. He carries me to the master bathroom, undresses me, and places waterproof cast protectors on my legs. He turns on the shower and waits for the water to get hot. He then removes his clothes and steps in with me. I sit on the seat and Phoenix lathers up my sponge and washes my body. I remind him that my arms are not broken and I could wash myself, but he indicates he wants to wash me, so I let him. I thank him for joining me as it makes me happy. After our shower, I slide on an oversized t-shirt and lie in the bed. Phoenix throws on another pair of jeans and button down shirt and tells me he will let me rest and he will see me at dinner. "I'll be in my study working on some major deals with building more ships," he mentions. "When you have time babe, I would like to know more about your business, your family, your childhood, and everything else about you." "You will know everything about me but right now I want you to relax. Please call me babe if you need anything," he says. "I will," I softly respond and he leaves the bedroom. I pull the covers up to my chin and drift off. My little nap is interrupted when Aunt Hattie knocks on the bedroom door to let me know dinner is ready. Phoenix comes in behind her to help me to my wheelchair. We make it to the dining room table where Ben and X are already seated. Phoenix helps me out the wheelchair and onto a dining room chair, he asks if I'm comfortable and sits next to me. All five of us enjoy the wonderfully cooked meal that consists of: smothered pork chops, fresh cut string beans, garlic mashed potatoes with gravy, and buttered wheat rolls. I am so stuffed I can't move from the table but want to lie down and watch my favorite TV programs. Aunt Hattie gets up from the table and starts to remove the dishes. "Is there something I can help with?" I ask. She says, "No sweetheart. I will load the dishwasher and we will relax the rest of the evening." I didn't argue with her and remained at the table until someone could help me up. Phoenix looks up and smiles and I ask him what is he smiling about; he tells me he is so happy and that he is truly blessed to have me in his life. I return the smile and think I should tell him about the conversation I had with Cameron earlier today. "Cameron called me today." "Why?" he asks. "I think he just wanted to ruffle my feathers and he did." That line that develops across his forehead when he's stressed appears in record time. I see the concern on his face as he asks, "What did he say, what did he want?" I explain that Cameron started the conversation with how he is getting help with his anger issues and that he knows in order to heal and move on he needs to call and apologize to me for the wrong he did to me. I told him I accepted his apology and thanked him for calling. He proceeded to tell me he was worried about me and that he heard I was in an accident; he wanted to make sure I was okay and was being cared for. I explained to him I was recovering well and thanked him again for calling. Cameron then flipped the script and went from being cordial to being the crazy person that he is. He told me he wanted to come to the club and see me one last time so that he would have closure. Needless to say, I told Cameron that it would be in his best interest not to show up at the club. I hesitated about telling Phoenix that Cameron knew details about my injuries and about the pregnancy and that he pretty much threatened me. I know if I didn't tell him and he found out he will be upset with me and I don't want this relationship to begin with lies. I tell Phoenix there's more. "Cameron pretty much threatened me by saying that he would hate if I had another accident and didn't make it or even worse if something were to happen to the babies I am carrying!" I don't think I have ever seen Phoenix get that upset. He jumps up and starts pacing around the room and speaking in a different language. Aunt Hattie asks if everything was okay. I assure her that everything is fine. She then asks, "Then why is he speaking in Russian?" I tell her he's fine and he's just letting off steam. Aunt Hattie informs me that Phoenix only speaks in Russian when he's really pissed off about something. "What's going on with the two of you?" She asks. Phoenix stops speaking for a second to tell his aunt it is not me he's upset with but the idiot who wants to harm me and our unborn children. Phoenix then calls X in the room and tells him they need to take a ride because he needs to take care of something. Aunt Hattie tells Phoenix that he and X will do no such thing. She says she knows he is upset and that he wants to make sure nothing ever happens to me or the babies but going out and doing something stupid will not protect them especially if he ends up hurt or in jail! And furthermore, he was not raised that way. "Let the police handle it Phoenix, they are best with situations like this. You know Detectives Watson and Kendrick are on your side and it's their goal to solve this case," she says. She also states that the police will make sure Sydney is safe, and they will put Cameron behind bars if he gets out of hand. "The last conversation you had with them, they indicated they had enough evidence to prove that the woman who confirmed his alibi was lying, so have comfort in knowing that they are close to bringing him in," Auntie Hattie tells him. Phoenix sits down on the couch in the living room and puts his head in his hands. He tells his Aunt that he absolutely cannot let anything happen to me or his children. He says in addition to her, we are all he has and he will lose his mind if anything were to happen to us. Aunt Hattie assures him that we all will be fine and the police will do their jobs and bring Cameron in when they have all the evidence they need to get him convicted. I ask Phoenix to come sit next to me. I grab his hand and lay my head on his shoulder. I tell him his Aunt is right and that everything will be alright. He turns to me and gives me a quick peck on the lips with tears in his eyes; he tells me he loves me so much that it will kill him if anything happens to me. "I love you Phoenix. I know that the babies and I will be just fine because we have you protecting us," I explain. He looks at me and expresses how happy and blessed he is to have me in his life and how excited he is that he's going to be a father. He says from the moment he saw me, he knew he would love me and now it's been confirmed that I love him and he's been waiting for me to tell him. I surprised myself by telling Phoenix I loved him which outside of my brother and Rocky I have never said that to another man. The love between Justin and I is very different of course and the love between Rocky and I is also very different. Justin is my brother and he has protected me from a very early age even though he is much younger than I am. He has always been my little protector and the love we share is like no other. Rocky and I have a special love for each other, again Rocky is like a brother to me and our love is special but a different love than that of which I'm feeling for Phoenix. I know that the love I have for Phoenix is real for the simple fact that saying "I love you" rolled off my tongue without even a second thought. The way he looks at me, the way he talks to me, the way he kisses me, and the way he makes love to me lets me know he is one of a kind and I thank God for sending this wonderful man to me! I just pray that I can keep him happy by being his wife one day and a great mother to his children. I pray that God gives me whatever it is I will need to accomplish this goal because he knows I am neither wife or mother material so I pray I can handle these major changes in my life because deep down in my heart I want this, someone to love me for me, to be someone's wife and mother of their children. I've always wanted this but I just thought this didn't exist for people like me, you know people who have had so much tragedy in their life, that if it wasn't for bad luck they would not have had any at all, and that would be me. But I guess God does answer prayers and I've learned it's always in his time and not in mine.

Chapter twenty-two

I hear Phoenix in his study on the phone with the detectives bringing them up to date with the most recent events. Phoenix is still clearly upset and I hear him say to Detectives Watson and Kendrick that he just wants them to do their jobs and catch the son-of-a bitch before he tries to hurt me again. Phoenix says he is not comfortable with asking me to be a part of a set-up, and that he does not want to put me in anymore danger than I have already been in. I'm still ear hustling when Aunt Hattie walks by and asks if I were hungry. "Shit" is what I say to myself, busted; I guess I will wait to have a discussion with Phoenix after his conversation with the detectives. Aunt Hattie has a nice cup of hot Jasmine tea waiting for me as I enter the kitchen. She tells me not to worry and that Phoenix will make this right, and for some reason I believe her. I'm comfortable that Phoenix has enough connections to make sure my case is the only case these detectives are working on and he will ride their asses to make sure they are doing any and everything to bring Cameron down. As for now, all the evidence is pointing to Cameron as I hoped it wouldn't because I wanted to give him the benefit of the doubt in knowing that he was somewhat a good person and that he would not be so evil as to do something so horrible to me by taking his car and intentionally running me over. But after the whole choking incident and the most recent conversation we had, I know deep in my heart that it was him and that he was in fact very capable of hurting me. Phoenix comes from his study and asks his Aunt for a cup of tea. He sits next to me at the counter and exhales. "What did the detectives say," I ask. He tells me that the detectives want me to call Cameron and tell him I changed my mind and I will agree to meet with him at the club after all. "Why do they want me to do that," I question. He says "because he is obviously in hiding and if you agree to meet him then he will come out and they can arrest him. The detectives will be in hiding and have undercover cops in the club in case something goes down; they will already be there with men on the inside and out, Cameron will have nowhere to run." Aunt Hattie says she thinks it's too risky and doesn't want me in harm's way. Phoenix agrees with her and said that the detectives are certain this is a sure plan to bring Cameron out in public so they can put him in custody. I think for a second and tell them both that I'm fine with it and will feel safe with undercover cops in the club and Rocky and X will be there as well so I will be well protected. Phoenix tells me he is still not comfortable with the idea but will go along with it as long as he will be there as well. I reach over to interlock his hand with mine and tell him I would have it no other way. I deleted Cameron's number a while ago but I think I remember his number. I grab my cell phone and decide to text Cameron instead of calling him. My text reads:

Cameron, it's Sydney, I've thought about your request of meeting me at the club so you can say your goodbyes

and put closure to our relationship so you can begin

your healing and move on. So meet me at the club

Friday night at 9:00 and we will talk then.

Sydney.

I guess I did have the correct number because within seconds of hitting the send button, I got a reply from Cameron.

Sydney, I'm so glad you changed your mind!

I'm really sorry I screamed at you over the phone the

other day, please forgive me! I will be at the club

promptly at 9:00pm. I can't wait to see you

Sydney, I love you! Cameron.

I look at Phoenix and tell him it's done, Cameron has agreed to meet me at the club on Friday at 9:00. Phoenix leans in close and kisses my forehead, tells me everything will be okay, and gets up and heads to his study. He calls the detectives to let them know that it's all set and Cameron has agreed to meet me at the club at 9:00 pm on Friday. I wake up Friday morning with butterflies in my stomach. I want to call Rocky and give him a heads up but the detectives advised against it because they don't want him to possibly give away what the plan is. I'm concerned because Rocky will not let anyone in the club that is carrying a firearm, so my question is how are the undercover cops going to enter the building with guns? I bring my concern to the attention of Phoenix and he tells me that's where I come in. I will bring the guns in the club in my duffle bag, I will be given a code that the cops will tell me so I know they're cops and can give them the guns at that time. How will I get alone with them with X and Rocky at the door? Phoenix tells me he will keep Rocky and X occupied until I am able to provide the undercover cops with their guns. "Can't X take part in this if I ask?" Phoenix says no because the detectives don't want him to know what's going on either. They do not want to compromise the set up at all by letting too many people know what the plan is. The only people who know of the plan are me, you, the detectives and the undercover cops. Phoenix expresses that the detectives are going against protocol and could be suspended or fired if anything goes wrong, but they are willing to take that chance to put Cameron behind bars. I feel a little sick to my stomach but I know I will be safe and I just want all this nonsense to be over with. I call Amber to talk to her; it's so hard not to tell her what's going on because if I did I'm sure she will blow the whole plan by showing up at the club. She would be so nervous and a pure giveaway that's something's up because she would never step foot in the club. I keep my mouth closed and don't mention a thing. She knows something is wrong, I guess she can tell it in my voice and she keeps asking me what is wrong. I tell her nothing and that I'm just really tired. She finally moves on and tells me about how's she's planning a romantic trip for her and her husband. She sounds so excited and I'm really happy for her. I tell her she deserves a romantic get-a-way and I'm sure her husband will be so happy and surprised. We talk for a little while longer then I inform her I'm going to go take a nap and I will talk to her later. I end the conversation with her and make my way to the bedroom to take a much needed nap. I get up from my nap still feeling a little tired and get ready to take a shower, I'm sure it's just my nerves getting the best of me. I begin to take my clothes off and Phoenix walks in the bathroom. "Hi baby," he sings. I smile and return his greeting. "How are you feeling?" He asks.

"I'm fine. I think my nerves are getting the best of me right now," I respond. "Baby you will be fine. Just be you and the plan will go accordingly," he expresses. "I have something that will calm your nerves if you're up for it," he smiles seductively. Woo-hoo, I think to myself. He hasn't touched me because I think he feels I'm too fragile right now. I return his seductive smile and reply, "I am up for anything and everything you have to offer." "Good," he says. He picks me up and carries me back to the bedroom, laying me on the bed; he stares at my nude body. He slowly starts to remove his clothes and I'm getting so hot and wet just looking at him. Once his clothes hit the floor, he crawls up to me kissing my feet. He laughs, "I will have to bypass your legs babe because we have some distractions," pointing at my casts, he says. I smile, arch my back and open my legs as wide as I can. Phoenix wastes no time in making his way to my 'centerpiece'. From the moment his tongue flicks across my clit, I want to explode. He comments on how wet I am and how he wants to be inside me. "And you will," I whisper. He continues to bring me pleasure by working his magic with his tongue. He knows I'm getting close because of my hip movement. He then slides his finger in me to massage my G-spot as he brings me to pure ecstasy. I explode! He tells me to turn on my side, I comply. After turning on my side, he comes up behind me and enters me from the behind. I take in a deep breath as I accept his entry. "Oh baby, I've missed you," I moan. He gives long, slow strokes as he kisses the back of my neck and then down my back and shoulders. Pure ecstasy is what I'm experiencing right now. I feel my inner muscles tighten ready to explode all over his manhood. "That's it baby, take all of this. Don't hold back babe, let it go. I have plenty more where that comes from," he whispers in my ear. I did just that, I let it go and I came so hard it scares me. Phoenix picks up the momentum and delivers hard thrusting strokes, bringing me there again. He tells me to hold on and let's cum together. I try but I can't control it, this shit is so damn good that I cum again twice before we cum together. "I miss you baby and you have the best pussy, it's addicting and I just can't get enough," he says with passion in his voice. I chuckle to myself because he sounds funny saying, 'pussy'. We both drift off for a well-deserved nap. I wake and Phoenix has disappeared. I move to get up to use the bathroom but my wheelchair is not near, "Shit," I said because it's in the bathroom. I yell for Phoenix and he comes rushing in the room asking what's wrong. "Nothing babe, I need to pee and my chair is in the bathroom." He breathes a sign of relief and helps me stand. We walk slowly towards the bathroom and I feel like a penguin walking. I shower and start to get ready for tonight's events.

I dress and eat to keep up my energy. Phoenix sits next to me at the table and stares at me. "What?" I ask. "Nothing, just checking on you that's all." "I'm good babe. Tonight will be another night at the club. Cameron will not have any more holds on me and we need to do this and be done with it for good. The butterflies have flown away and I got my game face on," I respond. Phoenix hugs me and says, "I know everything will be fine and that I have nothing to worry about because you will be well protected." He indicates he knows Cameron is not stupid enough to bring a gun to the club because he knows he will be checked at the door and he also knows Rocky will not put up with his shit, so we can be guaranteed he will not have a gun, at least not inside. The only guns in the club will be carried by the undercover cops, Rocky and X. "I'm not worried babe. It's all good and after tonight we will be able to move on with our lives without having to be worried about Cameron trying to hurt me anymore," I express. It's 7:00 pm and I am dressed and ready to go. Phoenix and I make our way down the lobby. As we exit the glass automatic doors, Ben is waiting for us with the back door open. We enter the car and make our way to Oakland. The club opens at 8:00 so there are only a few cars in the parking lot when we arrive, and those are the cars of the club's workers and dancers. On the way over Phoenix had a conversation with the detectives to go over the plan one more time. We come to a complete stop in the club's parking lot and wait for Ben or X to open the doors so we can exit the car. Ben makes his way around the car and stops at the trunk to retrieve my duffle bag and wheelchair. Ben comes around to let us out and I look over at the door and see Rocky standing at the club's entrance looking in our direction. Rocky has a non-emotional look on his face and I think to myself, I really don't want to deal with his attitude tonight! We exit the car and head towards the entrance. X places my duffle bag on my lap. We reach the front door and Rocky bends down to kiss me so I turn my head so he can kiss my cheek but he turns my head to make his lips meet mine, and kisses me. Not a passionate kiss, more of a smack on the lips, but inappropriate nonetheless. I brush it off and will address this little stunt later because right now I need to stay focused with what needs to be handled tonight. I look at Rocky as I'm wheeled through the doors and he has this very cynical look on his face, again, I dismiss it and will address it later. I greet some of the workers and dancers when I enter the club. I finally make my way to Delaney's office to get ready for the night's events. I left Phoenix and X at the door, so I know Phoenix will be executing his plan by distracting Rocky and X when this all goes down. I look at the clock on the wall and it seems like the time is going so slow. The club doors open in a few minutes and soon the place will be filled customers piling in. All of a sudden the butterflies in my stomach come back. I rub my stomach and tell the babies, "mommy will be fine and we will get through this together." They are my strength. I look in a hand mirror to check myself to confirm my shit is together...my legs might be broken but I still need to look like a bad-ass fierce bitch! My stomach is poking out just a little and I am wearing the pregnancy glow well. I leave Delaney's office to see what's going on in the club. As I wheel through the club I get a text message from Phoenix to let me know the undercover cops are sitting at the end of the bar to the right of the direction I was headed in. I look in that direction of the bar to see where the undercover cops are sitting and one of them tilts his head to acknowledge me. I then get a text message that reads, "Headed to the restroom sugar plum," one of the code words. I reverse my wheelchair and head back in the direction of the office and bathrooms. I leave the door to Delaney's office slightly open and the undercover cops follow in behind me and close the door behind them. I don't speak, I hand one of them my duffle bag and he unzips it. He retrieves 3 handguns and hands the bag to his partner who does the same. They place one under their shirts in the small of their backs, another under their jean legs and the last inside their blazers, probably in a holster. One looks at me and says, "Don't worry, we got this. Try to stay calm and go with the plan and no one will get hurt." He opens the door; they walk out and close it behind them. I take a deep breath, knowing it's all about to go down and I pray that this goes according to plan and that there are no surprises. I exit Delaney's office once again making my way back inside the main room of the club. Once inside the main room I stop by the bar to order a ginger ale. I sip my ginger ale and keep watching the door to see when Cameron arrives. It's 9:30 and still no Cameron; maybe he had second thoughts about meeting me tonight, maybe he got a tip that something was going down, I'm not sure what the deal is but his text message said that he would promptly be here at 9:00. I wheel around the club talking to some of my regulars and hearing how much they miss me makes me feel good. It's 10:00 pm now and still no Cameron. I send Phoenix a text message to let him know I am going back to Delaney's office to take care of some paperwork. He replies saying okay but the undercover cops will remain at the club until it closes just in case Cameron shows up. Thirty minutes later I hear what sound like gun shots. I place my pen down and go to the door and crack it to see if I can hear anything else. I hear people screaming and what sounds like chairs over turning. I hear more gun shots; I close the door and lock it. I go back to the desk to get my cell phone and try to text Phoenix but he doesn't answer; I try to text Rocky but he doesn't answer either. What the hell is going on out there? I ask myself. I am freaking out but I will not leave this office until I get a word from Phoenix or Rocky that it's safe to come out. I don't hear anything for what seems like hours, and then all of a sudden I hear what sounds like auguring. I want to go to the door and crack it so I can hear what's going on but I choose not to do that. I remain at the desk, away from the door and wait for some type of sign that it's safe to exit the office. My cell phone dings and it's a message from Rocky asking me if I was okay. I breathe a sigh of relief. "Finally," I say out loud, a word from the outside. I reply, "Yes, I'm okay just a little scared and wondering what the hell is going on out there." "Everything is under control, the police are here and it's safe for you to come out now," he responds. I still haven't heard from Phoenix thus far but I'm sure he's handling things out there and asked Rocky to text me to let me know everything was okay. I grab my phone, unlock the office door and exit Delaney's office. When I enter the club's main room I am faced with my worst nightmare. I see both of the undercover cops lying on the floor both with blood spilling from their lifeless bodies. I look over to the other side of the room to see X also lying on the floor motionless with blood spilling from his body. My body goes limp and Coco comes from behind the bar to my aid. I feel like I am about to pass out and I cannot breathe. I'm in search of Phoenix and Rocky. I look to the other side of the room and I cannot believe my eyes. I see Phoenix and Cameron on their knees with their hands tied behind their backs and Rocky standing in back of them with a semi-automatic gun pointing at their heads. I try to stand because I don't want to wheel myself over to him. I slowly walk in his direction using what tables that are still standing for leverage. I scream, "What the fuck is going on Rocky!? Why the hell do you have a gun and why are you pointing it at

Phoenix and Cameron!?" Rocky turns to look at me and with a very calm voice says, "Sydney sit the fuck down, we need to talk." I yell back at him, "I'm not doing a damn thing until you answer my fucking question, what is going on?"

Chapter twenty-three

Rocky chambers a round in his weapon and places it at the back of Phoenix's head; he tells me that unless I want to see my lover's brains all over the walls then he suggests I do what he says and sit the fuck down. My heart drops, I don't know what's going on and what might be going through Rocky's mind right now to make him act this way but I don't want to find out, so I sit down as he instructs me to. Rocky stares at me then blurts out laughing, "How could you have been so stupid to get involved with such a stupid ass fool like Cameron. You had to know that he was an idiot from the start, but your dumb ass could only see dollar signs and you were blinded from the reality of this fool being no good for you. Cameron yells, "Fuck you Rocky, untie my hands and put down the gun and we can see how bad your ass is then." Rocky takes the handle of the gun and smacks it across Cameron's head forcing blood to exit from his head. Cameron was already on his knees so he didn't have far to go to reach the floor; he fell to the floor and screams in agony. Rocky tells Cameron there's plenty more where that came from so keep talking and you're sure to find out. Phoenix calls Rocky's name to get his attention off Cameron. Rocky turns to Phoenix and again my heart drops, I pray, God please don't let anything happen to Phoenix. *You* just brought him to me, please...God don't take him away. I look at Rocky and scream his name. Rocky looks at me and says, "What do you want my love?" I ask him, "Why are you doing this? Why don't you put the gun down and sit with me so we can talk." He responds with a twisted look on his face that really scares me, "Sydney it's very simple. I love you and have loved you for years. But you were so blinded with all these distractions that you just couldn't see how much I love you. So I decided to take away all of your distractions so you and I can be together. And since you went and got yourself pregnant, I'll have to take care of those distractions as well." Tears are falling from my eyes as I explain to Rocky that I love him as well but he is like a brother to me and I don't see him in that light. He yells to the top of his lungs, "Sydney I am not your fucking brother! Why can't you see that I love you and want to be with you!? I was patient with you when you were with this loser Cameron and when he decided to choke your ass, who was there to rescue you; I was or did you forget?" "No Rocky, I didn't forget," I cried. "Don't interrupt me!" he shouts. "No, you don't interrupt me. You have always been there for me when I needed you and I love you very much for that but again that's because we have a close relationship and that's what friends do for each other, we take care of each other," I express. "Yes Sydney, we take care of each other but this so-called relationship is one-sided because I've been taking care of you for years and you keep running to the arms of other men, and for the life of me I can't understand why!" he howls. Phoenix says, "Rocky you are making a big mistake, you have killed three people, two of which were cops and if you give yourself up now they might go easy on you." Rocky turns to Phoenix and says, "You just won't shut up will you rich boy. Well I guess I will just have to shut you up myself." He's now pointing the gun at Phoenix. I scream for Rocky to stop but he raises his hand and comes down on Phoenix's head with all his might, causing him to fall to the floor motionless. Tears are streaming down my face uncontrollably. I beg Rocky to please stop this and it's me he wants, not them. "Please let them go so you and I can talk alone," I plead with him. Rocky looks at me and says, "I am so disappointed in you right now Sydney, I don't know what to do with you." "Why, why are you disappointed with me Rocky, what did I do now?" Rocky pulls up a chair next to Cameron and Phoenix and looks at me and tells me he has been patient with me and all my relationships with these men; and to make this situation worse, I go and get myself pregnant by rich boy over there. "What am I supposed to do now Sydney? I can't raise no other man's babies," he cries. I appeal to Rocky to please put down the gun and come over to where I am sitting so we can work this out. Rocky stands and thinks about it for a second, he's pacing the floor and sweating profusely. I can see Rocky is truly troubled and I don't know why I couldn't see this earlier. He agrees to put the gun down and come talk to me. Rocky makes his way over to me, then a voice comes from the outside blaring through the club. "We have the club surrounded and you have five minutes to exit the club or we are coming in." Rocky starts to pace again. "I will kill everyone in this club if you walk through these doors!" he screams. I beg him to let us all go so that we can end this and no one else needs to get hurt. I look over at Phoenix who is coming to, trying to focus his eyes on Rocky to see what he is doing. Phoenix calls out to me, "Sydney, are you okay baby?" "Yes Phoenix, I'm fine." Rocky says, "Oh how sweet, the love birds are concerned for each other's well-being." Rocky walks over to Phoenix and takes his cell phone out of his pocket. He instructs me to call Ben and tell him to back the car up close to the door because he, Cameron, and Phoenix are coming out and if the police try to stop him in anyway, he will shoot them. I did as Rocky asks; Ben answers on the first ring, I give Ben the instructions as Rocky gave them to me and Ben says okay he understands. Then Rocky screams for Coco to come here, again I plead with him not to hurt her as she has done nothing to him. Rocky tells Coco he is letting her go and she needs to tell the cops outside that he is coming out with Cameron and Phoenix and that he has instructed Ben to pull up close to the door so they can all get in the car and if the police try to intervene, he will kill these sorry-ass bastards. Coco is shaking and crying so much but I know she will do as she's told; she hugs me and tells me she loves me then moves close to the door. Coco reaches the door and turns to look back at me; she then says to Rocky that she cannot do this, she can't leave me. Rocky screams, "Have it your way bitch!" He points the gun in her direction and pulls the trigger! Coco falls to the floor. I fall to the floor and try to reach her. Crying and screaming, I'm asking Rocky how could he do this? "She's done nothing to you, she has two kids you asshole!" I scream! I am beyond scared, I'm pissed. I pull myself up and hobble in his direction. Phoenix is screaming at me to sit down and not to approach Rocky. I tell Phoenix, "I'm not afraid of this punk ass bitch! He has no balls or heart, he ties two men up who could take his ass out but instead he shoots a woman who could not defend herself. You ask me why I couldn't see that you loved me Rocky, oh I saw it but I didn't want to get involved with a weak ass man like you!" I said matter-of-factly! Rocky looks like he has steam blowing out his ears. "Sydney, I know you're upset and emotional and all because you're pregnant so I'm going to let what you just said slide. I don't want to hurt you because I love you too much, but don't fucking push me," he yells. He tells me he's going to take these assholes off my hands and we are going to take a little ride. I'm pleading with him to give himself up, but he ignores me and walks over to Cameron and helps him stand. He then helps Phoenix stand and points them in the direction of the club's entrance. He pokes the gun in their back to move them forward. Rocky tells Cameron to kick the door open with his foot and Cameron complies. The three of them had to step over Coco's lifeless body to exit the club. Ben is right there, he is close enough to the door and Rocky uses Cameron and Phoenix as human shields so in case the cops try to shoot him they will have to go through one of them first. They all make it into the car; Ben gets in the driver's seat, closes the door and tries to pull away from the front door. Ben gets basically nowhere when the car is surrounded by a multitude of cops. I'm trying to get to the exit as fast as I can. I make it out the door and scream for someone to get an ambulance. Much to my surprise they are already there and rush in to attend to those who have been injured. I hear one of the paramedics say, "There's a woman at the door with a gunshot wound to her abdomen! I need a stretcher!" he shouts. I pray to God that He saves her. Detectives Watson and Kendrick are there to help me. Another cop gets on the loud speaker and says, "Cameron, the car is surrounded, you will not get away. Give yourself up and let your hostages go." I look at the detectives and tell them that it's not Cameron, it's Rocky. They are both taken aback. "What did you say, did I hear you correctly Sydney," Detective Watson says. "Yes, you did. Rocky was the one behind all of this and has

Phoenix and Cameron tied up all because he says he loves me." "Oh great," the other detective says. I now hear the cop instruct Rocky to give himself up. Two other cops exit the club with a report from inside. I hear them explain that X and one of the undercover cops were dead but the other undercover cop was still alive and needs to be transported to the hospital immediately. Detectives Watson, Kendrick and I are now standing outside the club doors and I'm holding onto Detective Kendrick arm to help me stand. We are waiting to see if Rocky will exit the car and comply with the officer's request. I ask Detective Watson what's going on, she replies, "We're waiting a few minutes more to allow Rocky to give himself up before we move in." Detective Kendrick says he could not believe that they were looking at Cameron all along and the perpetrator was under our noses all along. "Who would have guessed that Rocky was the one who was stalking you and he was the one who ran you over?" More tears run down my face then my heart stops when I hear Rocky scream, "Sydney I love you and I'm doing this for us!" The first gunshot rang out from inside the car, then the second one, then the third, then the fourth and final one. "Oh my God please don't let this be happening," I pray. My body goes limp and I fall to the ground.

To be continued:

97555539R00124

Made in the USA
San Bernardino, CA
24 November 2018